WE BURN OUR DEAD

A Novel

TED LAUGHTON

This book is a work of fiction. All names, characters, dialogue, places, events, and incidents are a product of the author's imagination. Any resemblance to actual events or actual persons, living or dead, is entirely coincidental.

Copyright © 2025 by Ted Laughton

All rights reserved.

No part of this book may be reproduced in any form or by any electronic or mechanical means, including information storage and retrieval systems, without written permission from the author, except for the use of brief quotations in a book review.

Book Cover Design by ebooklaunch.com

For my family

1

There is a hillside by the sea, atop which sits only grass and dirt, a line of swaying pines along the far side of a seldom-trod road, a treacherous bluff on the other. The call of ocean waves comes muffled to the top of the hill, sea spray rising from the crags below, filling the air with pale mist and the mouth with brackish distaste.

Within the crevices of wet rock hide the delicate cliff-side nests of haggard seabirds, their tattered feathers ruffling as they struggle into flight, agile forms diving on bitter winds, desperate hunger driving them further out amongst a rising swell. Blind hatchlings huddle in the damp, not knowing where their mother has flown or if she will return, only that today they number three, when yesterday they had been more. The slap of tide against worn slate quiets their small voices and sets their hearts to trembling.

From the treeline rolls a different tide as languid fog slips from out the mouth of a sodden wood, slow-moving mist that snakes amongst the crowded trunks and through the snaring roots. There is life among the mute trees. The sudden rustle of leaf, a scratch of bark, the distant echo of a broken branch—all signs of a potent, if hidden, world. Hard seasons breed wary spirits, and the brief lives of others teach nothing if not the virtue of a quiet foot. It is a solitary life for such animals, but it is life—few are lucky to have even that.

And so to this place the warriors came, borne along the lonesome roads. Countless battles lay behind them, as many still to come—in between stood only waiting, and in that waiting, doubt. Thus the soldier seldom lingers, his sobering heart to the blood-drunk struggle always yearning. But even the sturdiest must some time set down weighty arms, if only to remind himself how hollow the ache of a hand without a hilt.

A few moment's rest was all they asked, but a single breath would do.

They would get not even that.

2

The warband moved on tired legs, following the rise and curve of the land, skirting the ocean cliffs as they went, leaving behind them the flames and the ash. They had no boats to take them away, their fleet and fortune sunk beneath indifferent tides, and so the sorry lot went now on foot, in silence and exhaustion, never grumbling, always moving, cursing the sea in every sidelong glance.

They moved as one, this company of men, a string of straggling figures, black-clad and empty-eyed, up the sea-slicked grass, on to another day, another night. None spoke, nor would any eye meet another, for these were the voiceless hours after the battle when soldiers moved beyond the reach of their fellow man, when the solitary reckoning must be made.

At their head walked lonely Sturmund, his broad shoulders stooped as he leaned into the climbing path. He moved slowly, one leg dragging slightly behind the other, the toll of battle exacting and cruel. As long as there had been wars to fight and lords to pay them, men to join him in his ceaseless cause, he had borne the mantle of command, ponderous as it was, without complaint. He would do so as long as he had strength to raise a shield and bear the sword—but he knew, as did his men, that a day was fast approaching...

Yet when that fatal hour should finally come, what glory there would be in the release.

Sturmund stopped, and thinking on that day, closed his eyes. The air was cool and wet on his burning skin, the taste of salt at his lips. The crash of waves against the rocks below were to his ears the crush of men against battlements, the cry of the lonely gulls like the wail of a dying man. War was all he had known, yet no one was made to fight forever. Sturmund was not afraid to die; he feared only dying poorly.

Behind him came the plod of boots, the scrape and clatter of plate and arms slipping to the ground, the sigh of restless souls. The line of men converged upon the crest of hill as their Captain stared out over a darkening ocean.

The white-faced stone fell for hundreds of feet, down to the churning waters of a blue-black sea. Sturmund balanced on the edge of the rise, the toes of his boots, the leather stained with earth and blood, hanging out over whistling air. When a single step could make an end of all toil, it is difficult to keep a man to the path. But mighty Sturmund never faltered, never so much as glanced at the tempting shortcut before him. His eyes, daunting in their measured calm, looked always forward, ever outward, searching for the day he knew would come. He meant to greet it when it did.

"Camp here, then, sir?" Marney's voice was flint on steel. Sturmund remembered the day the blade had taken the old soldier in the throat. He had never known a man to survive such injury, but Marney was of Northern stock. The cold winters of those icy lands bred hard men, perhaps none more so than Sturmund's second-in-command.

Sturmund nodded, his eyes still somewhere out beyond the restless waters. From the vantage, the entire turn of the coast could be glimpsed, the dark smoke could still be seen —a coil of ghostly gray and the faint glow of embers feeding on skeletal buildings and unburied corpses. Sturmund pointedly ignored the distant ruin. That was the wreck of yesterday, and Sturmund did not bother with such things.

Marney eyed his Captain with a crease, perhaps of worry, at his brow. But there were many lines and scars etched into the weathered face that it was hard to say for certain. His ancient eyes gave away nothing.

The old soldier turned and gave the order. The men began to unpack.

3

"Lucky it held up."

Patch perched on a rock, elbows resting on his knees, chin cupped between dirt-covered hands, looking every bit the vulture he was. He squinted with his good eye, the hollowed socket beside it covered by a scrap of soiled cloth.

He had set himself to watching Culp as the big man tended to his blade. A falling blow had bit deep into the metal's edge, and Culp traced the wound delicately. It was fortunate indeed that the steel had not shivered in the field. It was surely a ruined thing now, but Culp treated the sword with the reverence as befitted a fallen comrade.

"Although," Patch added, "losing your head wouldn't have been the worst thing to happen to your looks."

Several of the men looked up at this, little interest showing in their tired eyes, merely watchful of the outcome.

Patch had a word for everyone—seldom helpful, never kind. Culp, to his credit, appeared to pay the young man little mind, nor the few laughs the remark had garnered. He kept on with the rag and spit as he cleaned the blade

—all the while inching closer to where the vulture hovered.

"Looks kind of like your teeth, don't it?" Patch said of the now jagged-edged blade, screwing up his face and cocking his head for a more studied look.

Culp merely kept on with the rag, kept on with his inching, his heavy feet shifting idly on the grass, his face focused on his task.

"You're one to talk," Hull said from across the circle, his booming voice failing somehow to fill the odd quiet of their makeshift camp and the expanse of storm-blasted sky above. "I've seen old whores with better teeth than yours."

Patch cast a nasty grin at Hull. "And how is your mother these days?"

Culp seized his moment.

The heavy steel swished through the wet air, the flat of the blade lashing out savagely with a blow powerful enough to knock any man senseless—or worse, had it connected. But Patch was a veteran of more than one campaign, as was Culp, as were they all, and simple as the one-eyed fool might have appeared, his guard was seldom down.

Patch dropped his head, a deft little bob that suited the skulking figure on his perch, and the blade hummed clean past, cutting nothing but empty air.

The nasty grin began to form again on the dry lips as Patch lifted his head, but Culp, large and graceless as he may have seemed, was about, if not quite, as cunning as his prey. With a turn of his wrist and a quick shift of weight, Culp brought the arcing steel back the way it had come. With his full heft behind the swipe, the blade sailed twice as fast—this time with an aim for the vulture's blindside.

A baleful clatter broke the stillness of the hilltop as cold steel connected with solid bone. The flat of the blade curved around skull and rebounded, and with a sickening twang, broke at last along the weakened point.

Hull cackled as Patch dropped from his perch into the dirt. A growing stain on both sides of the man's trousers told them all just how deep into the dark Culp had sent him.

"It *was* lucky it held up," Culp said, eyeing what remained of his weapon. "If I could break this fine steel over your pudding head, just think what might have happened if I'd been up against a real man."

A senseless gurgle was all Culp got from Patch, but Hull gave him another ugly cackle for his trouble. The rest of the men had already gone back to tending to their equipment and, no less importantly, their feet.

They were tired, the lot of them, and for all the killing they had done that day, there was a need to express more than simple bloodlust. They had frustrations built up in their bones, an anger they couldn't place or satisfy on the battlefield that ate away at them nonetheless, a vicious cancer gnawing at their souls. Like a burst of steam from a roiling geyser, Patch had vented his self-loathing the best way he knew how—as had Culp, as would they all, in their own way and in their own time.

That was the way of it. Killing could make a man cynical, cause him to forget the worth of a life, only show him the futile and fragile way of things.

But then again, so could doctoring.

It was always the same—one man starting after another. It was as if they saw in each other something of their own natures laid bare, and it galled them.

Sturmund let them be, even if it meant more killing. It was no different than a surgeon bleeding a festering wound—if he didn't let them purge themselves of all the poison they had built up over the long days, there was no telling how far the infection might spread. Better one than many; better many than all—Sturmund understood this, and with a cold glance over the settling group, saw his hard philosophy once more affirmed.

The brief explosion of violence had served to steady the mood. When Patch woke, there could be a renewal, but more likely things would simply carry on as though nothing had happened, the pot taken off the heat, the boiling waters calmed, if still too hot to test.

"Hull, Patch." Thin as it was, Marney's voice carried with it the undeniable air of command, the hard-edge of a veteran warfighter who had no need to yell to let a man know he meant business. "Hunting detail."

"Sir." Hull rose, his heavy frame straining with the effort. The thick knots of hair, the color of rust and fire, coiled around broad shoulders. In truth, the hair was brittle and pale, faded by time and trial both, but Hull let the strands mat with sweat and blood so they appeared full and dark, as they once had—an old man's vanity, though one few dared remark upon. Hull may have had a good few years on the rest of the party, save perhaps Marney, but when things got thick, the old dog still gave as good as he got—and then some.

"Where's Patch?" There was a hint of surprise lurking somewhere in the wispy notes. Marney was not a man used to asking twice.

"Still out," Hull said, doing nothing to hide the smirk. Patch had not only pissed himself but, whenever the vulture finally did wake, he had an even more unpleasant surprise waiting for him in his trousers. Culp had sent the young man deep into the dark—when he should finally claw his way back to the light and the living remained anybody's guess.

Marney grunted his displeasure. For all of Patch's churlishness, he was by far their best huntsman—this despite his handicap.

"Ghost," Marney called. At this, Hull's smirk vanished.

"I can go it alone. I don't need that creature along with me." The pleading tones in Hull's voice only triggered Marney's more sadistic instincts.

"No," Marney said, the corners of his mouth turning up slowly, "we wouldn't want your old bones getting lost. Take Ghost with you. I'd rest so much better knowing you had some company out there in the wilderness."

"Aye, Sir," Hull said in defeat.

Hull took a slow breath. He could feel, if not hear, the soft tread of the paleskin's approach, and his stomach slithered in response.

"Sir." The ghostly killer spoke in a decidedly feminine way that Hull, in particular, found off-putting. The rest of the men chose to ignore this feature—as they ignored so much about the cursed man—but Hull found himself forever transfixed by the ghastly pallor of smooth flesh and what he took to be a demon glow in otherworldly eyes.

Marney smirked at the two men, standing at attention before him, and the sight gave him no end of pleasure. Hull loomed fully head and shoulders above the paleskin, yet Marney could practically hear the old warrior's toes squirming in his boots. The thought of sending the pair off into the darkening woods was a thing he and the rest of the men would laugh good and hard over while waiting for the two to return with supper. Until then, Marney's gut would just have to ache and bear it.

Their siege of the village had depleted most of their rations. The group preferred to travel light whenever possible, taking what they needed or wanted from others, scavenging and hunting when civilization was scarce. They had expected rich spoils from their most recent conquest, but the villagers had chosen to burn their food stores rather than give them up to raiders. It was a shortsighted and spiteful act, one that had introduced the villagers to the wrath not only of trained killers, but of hungry men.

"Come on, then," Hull grumbled as he trudged towards the treeline, but Ghost was no longer beside him. The old warrior looked around in time to catch a fleeting glimpse of a pale figure sliding into forest shadows.

4

The campfire roared in the sudden gust, the well-tended flames rising high, feeding hungrily on the open air, swirling like a vortex and throwing sparks as the damp wood within dried and cracked. From twigs or sodden leaves, Sturmund's men knew how to stoke a fire. It was one of the few skills they all shared, most of them excelling in some manner of war art unique to themselves, taken from their own people, handed down by their forebears.

Culp had his long blade, the whirling reaper of the battlefield; Patch his daggers, iron teeth that bit as cruelly as the young man's own tongue; to Hull, his unwieldy hammer, as unstoppable as the old warrior who bore it; Sturmund, his fists and sword, feared in equal measure. Ghost knew the ways of the shadows, and had earned well his name—he alone could speak to the forest, and even Sturmund deferred to the cursed man when their course took them through the wooded realms.

Marney read maps better than most, and knew the cultures and customs of many peoples. His knowledge had saved their band on more than one occasion, and few ever mocked the man for his bookish ways, when he alone could say which berry would nourish the stomach, and which would ravage the bowels. Nor was this to say the old scholar didn't know the right end of a spear. Throughout the long years he had proved his mettle, and he above all held Sturmund's trust, an honor more precious than gold.

For all their talents, motley as they were, every man to a one counted himself master of the craft of fire-making; but such mastery had little to do with the physical need for warmth, or even the simple desire to be dry. Sturmund's men often preferred the rain, and sat long hours under showering skies. When a man has felt another's slick blood dribbling between his fingers, it stays with him, long after the gore has been wiped clean. They knew no amount of rain could ever wash away the memories—still, they would try.

But not for warmth nor dry tunics did the warriors build their flames. The truth of the matter cut far more cleanly. For the art of fire-making, bringing light and heat into a dim and stony world, was one best appreciated by those sad men who knew what it was to fear the dark, those few who had done so much to increase its gloomy dominion.

So the men gathered round the ring of firelight, placing themselves well within its halo, and, turning their backs on the cold and the shadows behind, stared deep into the heart of the flames that writhed and danced before their weary eyes. The shapes huddled into themselves, each man drawing inward, craving comfort and solace, finding only himself and the wretch within.

Plenty of space was left between them, only four of them now gathered, Hull and Ghost off hunting, their Captain otherwise engaged. Like cardinal points on a compass face, the four sat sentinel by their stake of earth, guarding it and themselves with equal measure.

There used to be more—warriors. Now seven remained when once there had been dozens, scores, more. Gone was the age when a hero would fall, his kin rising to take up the mantle. It had become an age where dead was dead, immortality lost along with fatherhood. Glory, too, seemed a fading light. Their last campaign had taken the warriors through villages and hamlets scarcely deserving of the names. Few were the settlements with walls to defend them, fewer still with the men to man them. There was no honor in such victory, and the knowledge weighed hard.

What had happened in that seaside village—the ruin and the not-too distant flames—none cared to recall, even as the smell of cinder and strange meat crept up the trail behind them, following like the phantom it was. The growls of stomachs passed unmentioned, never unnoticed. Honor does not reside in a man's gut, only desperate hunger. They would spend much of the night burying the shame of that inglorious slaughter and the remainder packing down the dirt. By morning, it would be just another unmarked grave within the growing boneyard of their souls.

They were a storied lot, Sturmund's men, but the story was old and dim, tarnished with disuse, rusty from neglect, and that was the greatest dishonor of all—when to be forgotten was no different than never having lived. Great battles of their past looked with silent regard on the idle skirmishes of their present and beyond to the blind struggles of tomorrow. The warriors lived under the yoke of past glories, and one day, soon perhaps, would be crushed by them. But the men did not think overlong on such uncertain futures when that duty belonged to another.

Sturmund sat apart, in presence and in place, and in his

solitude seemed complete. Often was the evening he would drag himself to the edge of the camp and stare out at the night and the darkness it cradled. The men wondered, each to himself, what their Captain was looking for. Each held his own guess, different from the others, no more or less correct.

There were times when Sturmund joined his men by the fire, but those times were seldom. For all their respect of their Captain, the men were glad of his absence. His presence in the evenings troubled their already troubled spirits. A man could hide his face, shape the mask to fit a mood he himself knew nothing of, but eyes could never lie—and Sturmund's eyes were haunted.

There was a scuff of a boot from the darkness by the cliff, then of a stone sliding down into the far abyss, clattering against the rock wall as it fell. All four heads turned at the sound, four owls perched beneath their cloaks, breath steaming, eyes gleaming with fire. Somewhere in that dark their Captain stirred. But his troubles were his own. They each turned back to the fire, in their own time, and tried to forget, and for a time there was silence, save for the occasional cracking of a burning log.

One of the figures stood suddenly, rising silently, legs uncoiling gracefully. It dragged the cloak with it as it moved closer to the fire, the shadow thrown behind it long and looming. The other three remained motionless, their bodies tense beneath their blankets.

"Sit down, Bitch." Patch spoke plainly and with none of his usual bad temper, this despite the pain Culp had left ringing in his skull.

Still, the figure chose to force the issue, taking offense where none had been meant—not everyone had gotten the chance to purge their hurts that evening.

"Stupid, Patch," Culp said, and Marney added to the sentiment with a grunt.

It was not the name that had caught in her craw. Many years back, when she had first come to Sturmund and his men, seeking them out where they roved, she had presented herself by the same title and had worn it proudly ever after. She said she had been called such as long as she could recall, first by her father and countless men thereafter. It had never bothered her. After all, had she not put those same men beneath the ground, filled their mouths with dirt and their guts with steel?

It was not the name that bothered her; it was the presumption of command.

She walked over to Patch where he rested by the fire, squared up before him, and issued her own demand.

"Stand up, boy." Bitch glared down at him, her chest thrust out, chin raised, every inch of her bristling for a fight.

Patch gave one look to her, his good eye sizing up her terrible aspect, before dropping both the subject and his gaze.

Bitch looked down on him a moment more, spat to one side, then walked off beyond the reach of firelight and disappeared into the night.

Only after she had gone, her muffled steps receding into darkness, did Patch begin to breathe again. He fell back to nursing his head, grousing occasionally to any who would listen about his empty belly. Not even the shadows seemed to care, dancing blithely along the dirt, shapes wild in the firelight.

Bitch made the seventh and last of Sturmund's number, and her skill set had proved as wide-ranging as it was deadly. Preferring close combat to the crossbow she kept strapped to her back, she was, nevertheless, not choosy when it came to the slaughter. No matter how she brought death, from near or far, she brought it with the same awful certainty. It is always the bitch of any species that fights the most tenaciously, placing itself in the line of fire for the sake of its litter, bearing the most withering blows only to rebound with savage reprisal. There was no doubt in any of the men's mind whom the child was that Bitch fought for, even if it were only a memory.

Bitch was never shy in showing her scars, the silver-white strips of flesh that crisscrossed her stomach. The men who had dug the infant from her womb had no doubt caught Bitch unawares, and only on the most desolate and dreadful nights, when sleep eluded and mocked, did Sturmund's men ever give a thought to what wretched ends must have befallen such sorry fools. Bitch loved to tell of her kills, no detail too ruthless to recount, but on the subject of her child's killers, she remained ominously mute.

The three men, Patch not least of all, now revisited this unpleasant theme, wondering and doubting in equal measure, and above all, thankful that the warrior called Bitch fought under their same banner.

Above them the sky rumbled, and an icy drizzle began to fall. The men tugged their cloaks more tightly about themselves, and leaned closer to the hissing flames.

5

"You're going too fast," Hull called, a whisper far louder than had he simply spoken the words. "You're going to scare them all away." And at that, Hull increased his pace.

The old warrior lumbered through the brush with neither the grace nor the guile prerequisite a hunter, his heavy tread and labored breath drowning out the birdsong and alerting animals of their presence for miles around. His companion was nowhere to be seen, and had remained so much of their journey. Only the unusual stillness left in his wake gave any sign to Hull of Ghost's earlier passing, for though neither broken twig nor trampled earth marked his tracks, the hush of night—the cold, hanging emptiness—was as sure a sign as any that a ghost had happened by. Hull strode through the quiet, following the invisible path with growing displeasure, and put to death any lingering silence beneath the heft of his boot heel.

Hammer always at the ready, Hull had nevertheless begun to despair of their securing supper. He would blame Ghost, of course, and one dark part of him even hoped for their failure—hunger and a bit of shame seemed a fair price for bringing the paleskin down a notch.

The two had set out near dusk, with only the gloaming to guide their way, but in the denser parts of the forest, where day and night were one, no sunlight ever reached the forest floor. Hull was near blind in the darkness, but he knew such deficit would not hinder his companion, whose senses seemed only to sharpen in the shadows. Hull took this affinity for the dark as further proof of his companion's infernal predilection.

In the distance ahead, Ghost stalked. Hull could neither see nor hear the man, but he was sure of nothing if not the paleskin's eerie presence in the dense scrub beyond, where the treeline narrowed and the canopy thickened, and all manner of dark things lurked. It had been meant as a courtesy, though one Hull failed always to appreciate, for if Hull could sense his companion's presence, it was only because Ghost permitted him to.

"Blasted witch-man," Hull grumbled, thrusting the invective out into the darkness, where it landed soundlessly, swallowed whole by the leering shadows. More complaints followed, but they lacked the same conviction, the lateness of the hour and the absence of an audience robbing them of their pleasing sting.

The old warrior pressed on, wading ever deeper into the dark-green sea, through fields of bush and scrub so intense in color they appeared black in the dim light. Every move brought the soft hiss and rustle of wet leaves against the hide of his leggings; every step, the tug of roots catching on his boot. He staggered once, on a particularly tough snare, and for a moment, thought he might fall. The idea of slipping beneath the dense brush, prisoner to its suffocating, strangling tendrils, appalled him. Hull was a seafarer—forests made him uneasy.

Hull would never admit such, least of all to himself, but just as the black vines crept up the trunks of the ancient trees, so too had the steady crawl of dread begun its march up his broad back.

"Ghost." Hull chanced again the whisper, this time unable to mask the apprehension in his voice. His aged eyes wrestled with the cloying shadows that hung in the stale air, that draped themselves from every branch and drifted like haunting cerements in the gloomy wood.

At first, only silence and the darkness returned his call, an emptiness that weighed hard on the old warrior's nerves.

Then, a glimpse—something large, something pale. It caught in the corner of his eye, and he swung his burly frame to face it, thinking Ghost had somehow doubled back on him.

It was not Ghost. Not *his* Ghost.

He tightened a sweaty fist around the leather-wrapped haft of his hammer—a familiar grip, something comforting and solid in that desolate wood.

Hull's vision had been failing for years, and in the darkness of the looming trees, he struggled to make sense of the shape in the distance. The rationalizations came fast, and died just as quickly.

A stag, perhaps, Hull's mind told itself. But the proportions were wrong—terribly wrong. The stag had not walked the earth that could raise its head so high, nor stand on legs so wide that a man might walk betwixt them.

A moose, then; a bear, Hull argued.

Mighty creatures both, but even they should tremble in the shadow of such a beast as stood before the old warrior. The knowledge stung.

Hull's mind would not relent, for its own sake and sanity. A life of stubborn fight would not fail him so easily.

Had there not lived creatures overgrown amongst their own kind? Hull asked the darkness. Was not he, himself, such a case? Was not Culp, great, big bastard that he was, yet another?

True, true, said the darkness—though nothing like this. Pebbles to mountains; candles to suns.

Besides, the darkness said, what of the color? Paler than milk, like moonlight and bleached bone, almost radiant amongst the dark of the solemn trees. Show me the man who has ever seen such sights, and I will show you a madman.

Ah. The color.

And Hull recalled a long distant time, when he had known a similar sight, had glimpsed a similar skin.

The return was effortless, as though the old warrior had never left that long-gone moment, when he had been just a lad who scarcely knew which end of the spear to use. The frigid waters of the Northern seas, the stretching waves and unreachable horizon, and the vast, rolling shape in the fathomless depths below their hollow vessel—he had never told anyone about what he had seen that cold and lonely evening, and had thought to have buried the memory for all time. But the piles of bodies he had laid upon it in the long years that followed, the rivers of blood he had tried to drown the memory with—all for nothing, when at a single glimpse, the memory breached the surface of his thoughts, risen from the black depths, and with fire in its eyes, greeted him as an old friend.

It would have made a worthy feast—that was how the old warrior summed up the present matter, hunger and humor for a brief, blessed moment overcoming the horror of the truth. Yet even as the thought came, Hull felt the cold brush of his hammer as it fell limp against his thigh, as acceptance dawned.

White beasts, touched by the gods: guardians of the land, sacred, inviolate.

And Hull believed; a life upon the ocean waves had taught the old warrior more than his share of superstition and doubt. Though, for all the hard-won knowledge, it had never occurred to Hull to extend this same deference to his own pale brother-in-arms.

The creature before him had not moved. It stood as motionless and quiet as the dead trees around it, and its stillness, long and knowing, was terrible. Of its features, Hull could make out nothing, just the odd luster of its skin, and the great, looming presence of its form.

Like a wave against an aged vessel, fear sloshed in the old warrior's gut, and he crushed the hilt beneath his grasp, thankful for the pain it caused his hand.

The minutes passed, or perhaps only the seconds—it was difficult to say in the presence of the creature, whose very being seemed to defy the right order of things, such that time itself appeared to skirt its unearthly hide, its force of being bending nature to its will, and not, as was just, the other way around. And trapped within that strange pocket of hell, severed from the aid of his lifelong brothers, shut out from the sight of the heavens by the impenetrable canopy above, was one very tired, old warrior; and his troubles were great: he would not move, could not retreat, dared not approach.

The silence of the moment grew, its frenzy unheard, but not for one moment unfelt; like the building pressure of a kettle, the riled evening threatened to burst its restraints. Hull's face gave a twitch, the tug of muscle at one eye, the curl of lip and flare of nostril. Something was to break—the stillness of the moment, the fabric of Hull's mind, the bone of beastly skull under mortal hammer's crush. At that instant, it did not matter to Hull which, so long as the moment passed, anything for the piercing emptiness to relent.

The beast snorted, and Hull's heart gave way to pain, his mind to senselessness. The sound from wet nostrils was jeering and cruel, and found the old warrior where he trembled. A wild breath plumed in the bleak air, shrouding an already obscure beast.

On Hull's brow, pungent sweat beaded, the dried blood of his hair running, a salty drop of dirt and grit slipping over one bushy eyebrow and into his lashes. The hand he brought to his eyes was thick and calloused—a sudden movement, the work of a moment—and when the hand came away, the beast had gone.

Only darkness showed between the trees, the breath of the creature already faded into nothingness.

Shame burned on the ruddy face, hotter than any fire he had left behind that night in venturing into such forsaken parts. In the space of three unsteady breaths, Hull had convinced himself of his folly: no creature lived that was so large, so white, so silent.

The grave was snug with two memories now to bury, but the bodies fell just as easily into place. He chastised himself for the fool that he was, and counted himself fortunate there was none to have witnessed his disgrace.

Now, turning his mind and his sights to the distant path his companion had set off on, Hull readied himself for redemption. A belligerent grin cut its way across his broad face.

Iron muscles tightened, straining the leather of his

leggings, testing the hem of his sleeves. He coiled his body for the rush. The aches and the hurt accrued over hard and bloodied years did not vanish in the exhilaration. When he bent, his tendons clicked and pinched; when he flexed, his elbows burned and strained; in his neck, the tension brought bones together and tears to his eyes. And Hull relished the sensation, for it only reminded him of how much he had taken, how much he had given back in turn. The pains fueled him, fed his own fires, drove him onward with implacable ire.

Wide and blind swung the hammer as Hull rushed his foes, the forest and its dwellers, the shadows and their secrets. In his broad, beating heart, he hoped only to land a blow against something living, that he might prove himself once more the master of the only hunt that mattered.

The forest had ideas of its own.

Within the distance of a few lunging strides, Hull was made to bring himself painfully to a halt, his knees throbbing with the sudden exertion, heels digging deeply into tender earth. He watched, breath caught in his mighty chest, as the forest came alive.

Movement everywhere—under foot and high above, in the distant shadows and points closer still, just beyond Hull's reach.

All around him, near and far, the brush erupted with the cries of the damned, all manner of shriek and yelp and hopeless wail filling the air with the many voices of death.

There came alongside that gruesome din the rustling of leaves and snap of twigs, the scratch of claws and chatter of teeth—and lost in that strange forest, amidst the lamentations of the wretched, Hull believed once more in gods and monsters. The graves of his mind spilled forth their demons.

"Come on, then, damn you!" The hammer raised in

angry grasp shook defiantly in the face of chaos. "Come get what you've been craving."

But even the lungs of the old warrior, so practiced in their raucous habits, were found, at that fatal moment, wanting. The mad and mindless prattling of dying souls drowned out the challenge completely, and left the old warrior a confused and pathetic sight.

Then fell the silence—all at once, as though the very air had been taken from the wood, a suffocating grip all the more unsettling for the vicious turmoil that had come before.

And from that silence emerged Ghost, arms laden with kills, placid grin stretched across his smooth face.

A ragged breath slipped from deep within Hull's broad chest, and no sooner had relief washed over him than anger began to boil. "You damned witch. I thought you were—" But he caught himself.

Ghost walked straight up to Hull and stood there expectantly. Hull gaped at the bounty—squirrel and mouse, rabbit and fox, at least a dozen lean bodies, though more than enough for that night and the next. With a final crush of the hilt, Hull lowered his hammer slowly, begrudgingly, and strung it on the notch of his belt.

Ghost dumped the carcasses into the old warrior's arms. Most of the animals had had their necks broken, some their throats slit. Dark blood smeared Hull's chest as he struggled with the load, animal heads lolling, an occasional twitch from the settling forms.

"Good work flushing them," Ghost said, violet eyes unblinking. "Big and stupid works. Sometimes." He reached up and patted Hull's cheek.

Hull watched, stunned, as the figure glided past. He had to struggle to catch up before the paleskin disappeared again. He did not wish to be alone, and for once was glad of the company.

Giving one last look behind him, around him, Hull saw nothing but ominous shadows, lurking dark. Even then the memory had begun to fade, though the fear still lingered—and perhaps always would.

The clouds opened then and began to piss on Hull as if they had been waiting all evening for the right moment. Hull shook his head, found a quiet chuckle hiding somewhere inside his burly frame, and hurried off after his companion. Where Hull caught each drop on his steaming skin, Ghost seemed only to move between the falling rains.

SHADOW DANCE

The evening stank of piss and blood; the ground was wet with both. There would be no escaping the stench. In life, there never was.

"We're priests, now, are we?"

Hull had been griping ever since they'd left the tavern. It had taken Culp and Patch both to drag the man from his cups, but now that they were out of doors, nose to the hunt, the old warrior had started to warm to the idea of a holy quest.

"We are warriors," Culp said, indignation quavering on his sonorous tones. The big man held no truck with gradations; he had labored under the impression that their task was as direct as locating the mark and introducing it to the sharp end of his steel. The moment life became any more complicated than that was the day Culp parted ways with his brothers-in-arms. That day lay years off yet.

"Yes, Culp," Patch said, as to a child, and a slow one at that. "You warrior. You stab-stab." He made playful jabbing motions in the air at Culp, but didn't actually dare prod the man. He had some sense, after all.

"Then why does he call us priests? We are not priests." The color was rising up the bullish neck.

"He was only jesting, Culp. He simply meant—"

"Don't answer fer me, boy." Hull glowered. "I know what I meant." And with that, the old warrior trudged off, Patch left to puzzle out the insult he had not intended.

Culp, too, gave the shoulder to Patch, this a literal one as he lumbered past.

"Such delicate flowers," Patch said, rubbing the tender shoulder.

The group walked on in strained silence, down alleys slimed with shit, watching their step and turning their attention back to their hunt. None could deny the presence that had joined them that night; the hairs rising on their neck spoke to their unseen guest. The difficulty would be in drawing out their prey. Patience, focus, cunning—all invaluable assets to the skillful warrior, all needed for their current quest.

"So what did he mean?"

"Oh, for the love of—" Patch had never any patience for his less gifted companions, in whose number he counted all but himself and, on his most generous days, Marney.

"He never said!" Culp's face was turning crimson, which, like the red sky to the sailor, was a sure sign of violence nearing. Culp had mastered many skills; restraint was not among them. Once unsheathed, his temper, like his blade, was never put away unsatisfied.

Patch eyed the threat. There was no doubt someone was getting smacked. Then or later—a smack would be had. He would need to do much to ensure that the censure fell upon another.

"I just meant," Hull said, stopping in his tracks and swaying from the ale, as if the road had carried on without him, "that now we're demon hunting—not people hunting, or even *Kura* hunting." *Kura* was the word Hull used when he meant something less than human and utterly expendable; no one knew from what language it descended, or if the red warrior had simply made it up, but it had joined the argot of their crew, tossed in with myriad colorful turns of tongue that made up their patchwork vernacular.

Culp's stony features only belied his difficulty following, but to belabor the issue further would be to invite the true sharpness of Patch's edge. Culp would never let the little shit know how much his barbs stung, so he simply nodded, and fooled none.

"Demons are work fer the priests, eh?" Hull said, with surprising forbearance. "That's all, I meant. But if the scrawny-old, virgin-fondling, god-humping gits can't handle their load, well then I guess we can shoulder the burden... fer a bit of what's in the coffers. So here we are—priests fer a price."

"Bless me, father," Patch said, with a snigger, "I've been a naughty boy."

Hull loosed a lecherous laugh. "You have, at that. I saw what became of them tavern girls. There's a pair that won't be smiling anytime soon." Another laugh followed, a wicked coda.

Meanwhile, in the distance, the scuff of foot against shingle passed unheard.

"I always thought I might have enjoyed being a priest," Patch said.

"And I shoulda liked to have been born a seat cushion in a fat woman's bedchamber. I'm not sure which is more ridiculous."

"It's no jest. All that power, all that respect." Patch sucked at his bottom lip.

"You couldn't diddle anyone. Not allowed."

"You *shouldn't* diddle anyone," Patch said. "But who's to say? One of those buxom church wenches comes crawling for forgiveness, just begging to tell daddy—I mean, Father—all her sins." He threw up his hands, showing how little chance the blame ever had of sticking. "Can't be helped."

"They have church wenches?"

"It's what they're known for, Hull," Patch said, scoldingly. "That and the wine."

"Well, what stopped you, eh?" The way of the cloth was beginning to sound rather appealing just then as Hull traipsed through a cow-pie in a land without cows.

"In the end," Patch said, sighing, "it was all just too much cant."

"Ah, they're all a bunch of cants, if you ask me."

"Quiet, the both of you." The voice was not pleasant, for it had never aimed to please. Bitch eyed the men with distaste and distrust.

"You hear that, Hull?" Patch said. "The missus wants that we should hush our tongues."

"I wish that someone would cut it off entirely," she shot back, eyes begging him to press his luck.

If Patch did not perceive the warning, it was not his visual deficiency to blame; he simply had no skill at gauging limits. It was, in part, why he was so very good a killer, and so very poor a man.

"I can think of one task that might occupy my tongue, if you like." The vulture-eye gleamed. "But I don't think it'll make the night any quieter."

Another volley burst from Hull's broad chest; Patch merely grinned. Neither saw the shadow slipping along the rooftop.

By chance or some deeper awareness, Culp looked up to

the rooftops, to where a nameless shape had stirred a moment earlier. The shadow had gone, and who was to say it had ever been there? Bitch was too much irritated to worry about their absent mark, when she had two perfectly good targets trudging at her fore.

Bitch had come to them only short months before, and in that time, had seen nothing to commend them to her cold, dead heart. They were proficient enough killers; but there was nothing new there. The world was full of men who could kill—and women.

They were four that evening, an unwieldy number, even for such an unusual contract. Three would have sufficed; two could have managed; four was merely asking for a fuck-up, especially in a group whose members could scarcely stomach their own company.

Was it any wonder then that they were already turned about in the dark and the filth of the crowded town, these battle-hardened killers who had not yet even realized that it was they who had become the hunted?

But it *was* a peculiar contract, and they could hardly be blamed for taking to their charge with something less than their customary ruthlessness. When the flesh of countless men had yielded so readily to their hungry blades, what chance did the subject of some fireside tale stand? They would be happy to act the part, to pocket the coin and let the townsfolk believe themselves saved from phantom threats.

Bitch was not surprised that superstition should abound in a town with more money than sense; wealth, after all, had a way of sickening the soul more easily than any pestilence. Full larders were always a sure sign of weak and idle minds. She was merely taken aback that their band should be the desired means of the town's salvation. She would have thought reputation alone might have kept the petitioners at bay. Word of their deeds had grown; to be recognized on sight for one's slaughter, that was a laurel Bitch struggled to wear, though her companions had little difficulty in donning the thorny crown.

The alderman had risked more than his repute in bringing the matter to Sturmund, but only the Captain could steer their course; if he wished to have his bid considered, the alderman had to lay it before the man himself—if he could find him, that was.

The others had obliged the official, had pointed him the way to their warrior-king. The politician had thought them rude, but the upward fingers they thrust at him did, indeed, show the way.

The inn, like most of its kind, was of two parts. On the first story, the tavern; on the second, the rooms. One floor, seedy; the other, simply debauched. Sturmund had taken the entire upper floor. The Captain was not niggardly with their spoils, and spent their gold well. He, himself, had nothing on which to spend beside his men, and earned again with gold what he had already attained a thousand-times over with his peerless command—their respect.

But Sturmund detested the cities, and had he another option, would not have stayed within the cramped and crumbling walls for all the wealth in the kingdoms. As it was, however, the cities were where the action was to be found. Sturmund, above all men, craved the fight—lording over it was his gift; wading into it, his passion.

It had taken the alderman some time and a great deal of frustration to find Sturmund's quarters. It was not that the inn was so very large. In the space of a few feeble heartbeats, the official had taken stock of the rooms; those that were empty, those that were impressively full. But in none of them had the man found the one described to him—not until he chanced to take the one-eyed scoundrel's advice at least halfway literally and fucked-off out the window.

At the top of the inn, as on the top of most stone buildings of that particular town, the roofs were flat and lined with slate. The sun baked them in the morning, and the residual heat warmed the structures well into evening. Still, it was an unusual place to find a man dreaming.

But Sturmund had not been dreaming. If the alderman saw as much, it spoke only to a limited mind. Sturmund was training, always. And on the slates he laid his back. Bare and bared, his body was his weapon, the sharp midnight air like a whetstone. Under its icy nails, the warrior's hide tightened, hardened, the muscles etched as though from granite.

The alderman had approached, unsteadily both for the terrain and the company. The conversation was brief.

"It haunts the town," the alderman had said.

Sturmund had no time for poetry. His eyes remained closed; he struggled to maintain his evening focus.

"You wish it dead?"

The alderman nodded, foolishly. Sturmund must have heard the clicks of the rheumy bones, for he answered straight away.

"Then go kill it."

A hasty step forward at the impertinence, but was it the wind or the warrior-king's burning presence that drove the wizened official back?

"Does it steal?" the Captain asked.

"Who can say? Bread, perhaps. Some fruit."

"But you have never seen it steal." It was not a question,

and the alderman, for all his faults and inadequacies, did not miss the point. His impotent silence spoke for him.

"Does it harry your people? Does it come for your women?"

"A dozen soldiers lie out in those fields this very night," the aldermen said, pointing to the fog-shrouded range beyond the humble walls, though Sturmund did not deign to look. "Under earth and stone."

"Soldiers thrown at a bashful demon. Yet you call yourself slighted?"

"These were men, not beasts to be chucked and forgotten."

"Men scarcely deserving of the title," the Captain said, "to come in number for a fleeing foe. With what provocation? Your shadow is a ghost not a demon, and a ghost is a thing already dead. I have no use for such creatures."

The alderman's face was flushed. "I have money."

"I have gold enough to drown you and your town."

The alderman wished to laugh, but the bearing of the man before him, so regal, so strict, would not permit it.

"It stalks our town, our nights, our rest. Its purpose may be obscure, but it can not be but fell. These were our best swordsmen—"

"What does it look like?" Let him but hear the talk of the town, the tall-tales of drunken men, of frightened fishwives, and he very well might hasten the alderman the quickest way off the roof.

But no description was forthcoming.

There stretched a very long, very unequal silence between the two. Where the alderman floundered in the stillness, wishing only to fill it with comforting prattle, the warrior inhabited it—wore the silence, bent it to his will, became it.

"You have never seen it." A question lay in the stony voice, a hope that dared not rise to eagerness.

"*No one* has seen it." The alderman thought nothing of his shame as he spoke, and everything of his fear.

The Captain did not need eyes to know the man's terror; he could smell the stench clearly enough. This one was terrified of everything, of his position, of his own people, to say nothing of demons and the killers he wished to hunt them. Sturmund quelled his distaste for the man long enough to decide the course.

Something no other man has managed, to kill where others had quailed—their company claimed such distinctions with each passing battle. Even as their numbers thinned, their repute only grew.

A prey unseen, cunning as the night—Sturmund had known Patch to disappear entirely into the trees, bow in hand; very recently, the Captain had been surprised by the young rogue dropping from some hidden branch, down from the steep elm that overlooked the convent bathing pools, glow on his face and stain on his trousers.

A demon that has slain a dozen men—Sturmund might have laughed had he remembered the way. Even old Marney could still skewer as many; and at the throw of a single spear, Sturmund would wager.

But that, of course, was Marney. One of Sturmund's men. A warrior.

And yet, it had not always been so.

Marney had walked many paths, lived many lives, before joining the ranks of the damned. Had the old soldier not begun his life but a humble scholar, content with tome and quill, delicate fingers stained with nothing more than ink? But when the call came, how readily the unassuming scholar had traded quill for spear, the histories he wrote to be etched in blood from that fateful day onward.

Trace back a warrior's path far enough, and if one did not get lost in blood and bone, one would find it always the same: the nameless child, the humble beginnings, the fertile soil from which grew the man. The waifish lad, Marney the Scholar, the same reckless soldier who had scaled the Citadel's battlements and brought a swift and merciless end to the Usurper within. There are no short paths to glory, but there are opportunities aplenty. All that is needed is the will —and the vision.

There was something to that; and no surprise it was through Marney's own example that the Captain should come to understand such. Perhaps Sturmund had grown spoiled in his slaughter, thumbing his nose at the chance to greet new company, face new challenges.

There was nothing to lose, Sturmund knew, except his life. The realization cheered him some, and the Captain's eyes opened.

The grip of that glacial stare, the awfulness of its purpose, almost drove the alderman screaming from the rooftop. But the same dread potency that threatened to run him from the ledge also rooted him to the spot.

"We will find your shadow-man." The eyes closed, the ears with them.

The petitioner rambled a few moments more; like the headless chicken, the habits of the political creature linger beyond good sense. Sturmund had heard all he needed.

∼

The order had came down through the ranks: the hunt was on.

Marney had been first to volunteer, perhaps the most telling sign that strangeness was in the air. In truth, the mere mention of apparitions and demon lights offered more than enough inducement for the old scholar to leave his fire and his books, if only for an evening. But Sturmund came to his second, not in private but before any eyes that wished to see, and shook his head—as simply as that. Marney deferred without debate and set himself back to his studies.

That was the way of it, not just for Marney, but for them all. The Captain's company, the Captain's call. There was no slight in the decision, nor could there ever be when only truth was spoken.

Sturmund prized Marney's wisdom, which was why he would not risk so valuable a resource on so uncertain a venture. What knowledge Marney might possess, he could share before the party set off. As it happened, there stood an even bigger responsibility in need of managing, and only one of Marney's prodigious talents would do.

Sinner and Strange Bob had been at each other's throats all evening, Bob's penchant for waxing lyrical at the most inopportune times wearing down even Sinner's infinite patience. The situation wanted looking after. Were the two able to walk, Sturmund would have surely dragged along the wild-eyed pair to work out the kinks between them. As it was, they could barely shit without help, on account of the poison tearing up their innards and eating away their minds.

But that was nothing new; more curse than poison, the corruption had been with the two as long as any in the company could recall. It was only when the moon rose queer, as it had that evening, that the troubles boiled their way to the surface.

But that was Marney's problem for the night, and Sturmund had absolute faith in his second. He gave no further thought to what were sure to be busy hours at the inn, certain the grizzled lieutenant would know how best to manage the two shitting madmen. And so, mop in hand, Marney watched them go—the four-man party setting off into the night; his Captain stalking off in a different direction and with a different purpose altogether.

An hour later, and only a few hundred yards from the doors of the inn, the party realized its situation—the town was a warren. Unlike the wooden structures of the South, the stone buildings of the Coast were built so closely upon one another that it could not be readily determined where one tenement or tavern or hall stopped and the next began. More often, the ancient clay and shale, laid down long ago by some forgotten forebear's hands, would slide and settle, shift and reroot, so that over long years the two masses of stone and mortar would become one. More deaths occurred from property disputes in the coastal townships than in most civil wars of the Eastern provinces combined.

That same architectural eccentricity now posed a deadly challenge to the hunting party. Nowhere in the entire town did two lines ever run parallel—that went for roads, walkways, walls, and roofs. The distorted geometry of the alleys and thoroughfares was dizzying; at night, it was maddening.

"We've been this way before," Patch said.

"How the hell would you know that?" Hull had sobered considerably over the past hour, and his temper had worsened in equal measure.

"See that puddle, right by your foot?"

Hull looked down at what he stood in.

"That's where I pissed five minutes ago."

The red warrior sighed. The long beard, where it fell below his chin, was wan as straw from where the sloshing ale had washed away its bloody colors. He cut a careworn figure despite his hearty frame. An hour of uneven cobbles and progressively narrowing alcoves had taken its toll on them all, their heftiest man not least of all.

"Can we just, fer fuck's sake," Hull said, exhaustion tempering the fire, "find this shadowy shit and be done with 'im?"

"If you two hadn't been running your mouths all night," Bitch said, cutting off Patch before he could add one more piece of useless trash to the already fetid air, "we already would have."

And of course, Bitch was correct. No huntsman would ever intrude his footsteps, let alone his voice, into the arena, as they had that night. The prey is always wiser, always quicker of foot and thought—it is a fact universally known.

Dust sifted from the lintels at Hull's passage; bitches of every sort perked up at the lechery in Patch's tones. Even Bitch and Culp, so well disciplined, and who might never have uttered as much as a sigh had they been sent out just the two of them, found themselves constantly rebuking their companions, their own resolve utterly overwhelmed in the face of those two hobgoblins of chaos.

As it stood, not one of their number had heard the myriad scrapes and scuffs, the chip of shingle and the creak of roof beam, the fell tread of that which had pursued them through the night, that had followed from above, that lurked even then just out of sight, and only scarcely out of reach.

"And where is Sturmund?" Patch complained loudly. "Where is the fearless leader tonight? I thought he was supposed to be helping."

"Mind yourself, boy." Culp would not suffer disrespect of his Captain.

"Oh, pardon me. I forgot you were his bum-chum."

"You filthy little pig." This time Bitch had heard enough. At least one thing must be kept sacred; the torch she bore might one day burn her to cinders, but just then she would use it to scorch out a scoundrel's last eye.

The nails were sharp as any dagger blade, and thrust in such a straight and practiced strike, would have surely pinioned the eyeball clean in its socket.

Once bitten; twice shy, however—Patch had no intention of letting another cunny snatch something so dear to him.

The nails came close to their prize, but Patch reacted like a thing scalded when he saw the true intention behind the lunge. Wild, crazed, his agile frame seemed to fold back on itself, his torso bending painfully, desperately, as it took his head out of range of the blind and blinding fury.

The snarl on his face was reflexive, instinctive, as befitted so feral a thing. The impulse to maim, to kill, came quickly to his mind, and would have been just as quick to his hands had not Hull broken their combat with a cry.

"What in the hells is that?"

All turned to look at what the red warrior spied. It was a wonder any of them had missed it. Bitch and Patch set aside their violence, bottled up their fury for another night each was sure would come soon enough.

High above them, from the heavy darkness of the rooftops, gleamed a demon's eyes, jewels in the darkness, beautiful, deadly—blue.

"A witch," Hull said, readying his hammer for the throw. A dangerous brew of anger and revulsion had mixed in his bulging gut.

"No, you fool," Bitch said, staying his hand. It took her entire body wrapped around his arm to stop the hungry momentum.

Culp lowered his blade and then his head. "Captain," he said respectfully.

The others echoed the salute; Patch as well, if only as a murmur.

"What are you doing here, sir?" Bitch looked up at him were he perched on the ledge. She was glad to see him; though the warmth she felt at his presence would always be a thing wary to her.

"I shame of you all." The words did not come angrily, and for that stung more sharply still.

No one spoke. No one had the words, for there were none.

"I send you out to catch a shadow," the Captain said, from his shadowed perch, "and you can not even spot mine as it walks along with you." It was the eyes that spoke loudest, the icy fields growing colder still.

"What would you have us do?" Patch spoke as only he could, with words perfectly reasonable, and so dripping with contempt.

"Exactly as you have done; exactly as I had thought." He stirred, rising carefully on the uneven slate. It always surprised them how graceful the great warrior could be; many foes had died with much the same thought. "You have flushed the shadow; I have traced its source. When any prey is harried by such loud and clumsy trackers," here Patch's pride thought to object, but Culp's iron grip on his shoulder caused it to reconsider, "it will look to the peace of its burrow."

Sturmund pointed with his sword, the blade directing them to something well beyond their line of sight, above the mud-stained walls and crumbling foundations. They would need to join their Captain on the rooftops to know for certain.

Bitch and Patch were up the walls as lighting, while Culp and Hull both understood that they would need to take their companions' word on the matter; the roof had not been built that could support such two as they. And from the higher vantage, the three keen-eyed trackers saw.

It moved like nothing Patch had ever known. As subtle as sin; as silent as the moon. They watched together as it slid ahead of them in the distance, dancing on the black air, bounding the gaps between buildings, caring nothing of the roads that lay between.

Sturmund was correct; its movements were not meaningless. Though the shadow darted and leapt as if compelled by wild chance, the path it took led it on in one constant direction. In the far-flung corner of the town, the building stood. No great tower, nor decaying castle—this was no demon's keep. Just a structure as old as what lay about it, though made all the uglier for the clear disuse that had befallen it.

As the shadow reached the building, having flung itself across a great divide from the crumbling structure opposite, it paused, straightened, and turned.

The moon, so long demurring that night behind ashen clouds, peered long enough from out her cover to cast a wondering glance at the world below. In the delicate light that traced dreamily across the rooftops, the company saw what it was they hunted, and knew from that moment on it was no mere shadow.

The milky form dimmed with the passing light, the violet eyes gleaming once before extinguishing. It saw them, as they saw it.

Turning mutely, the figure disappeared into the inner dark of the silent building and waited.

Patch's silence spoke for them all. Hull jostled his one-eyed companion for the details when the lithe figure lighted back to ground, but the young man remained mute. After all, what more could words express that the moon had not already put so elegantly?

They had their bearings, and for the first time that evening, continued in a silence mindful of the empty noise that had so long preceded it.

When they reached the doorway, they each took a last look at the darkened sky, hoping for just a glimpse of light before charging into such obscurity, but the moon would not share her grace a second time. They needed no further sign; they slipped within.

It was an austerity to take even Sturmund aback. Of what his straining eyes and groping hands could perceive, there was nothing to the meager space but shadows and cracked tiles, bare walls and empty hearth, damp air and mocking echoes. The hardness of so crude a shelter in so rich a town brought a strange swell to the Captain's breath, perhaps pity, perhaps approval, informing the emotion; in the utter blackness of the hovel, the gesture passed unseen.

As for Patch and Hull, Bitch and Culp, for all their many failings that evening, they met the darkness unmoved, fanning out silently, minds only on their murderous task, and in doing so, reclaiming the full regard of their Captain. How the darkness felt at their arrival remained to be seen.

A shadow peeled itself from the far wall. None had seen it, for it waded soundlessly into waters just as bleak, the heady darkness of the room a pool in which they all now struggled to keep abreast.

The blades of the ones who had come were all drawn.

That was a mistake, the shadow knew. Even absent light will find a careless edge; it watched the dull glint of steel floating in the emptiness. As for itself, it would not unsheathe its own blade until the fatal moment.

Bitch stared into the angry dark, seeing faceless forms she knew were not really there. Behind her, the shadow poised. Not even the hairs of her neck had sensed its approach.

The blade fell.

The shadow had accounted for their positions, for all of their awkward placements throughout the narrow room. It knew where each blade loomed; where best to roll away after this first slice; how best to reengage. It was not the first time killers had come to call.

For all that, the shadow had not accounted for the brute.

By unlikely chance or some strange magic, Hull had managed to trip himself up in the darkness. This odd feint, the shadow had not foreseen, a grown man downed by his own boots. The burly frame came on, drawn by its own ponderous weight. The blade-arm fell diverted, the crashing huddle of bodies struggling to make sense of themselves.

Like a spark to black powder, the mayhem lit off.

Six blades shining in the darkness, clashing blind and carelessly. So much skill carried the weapons, but so little thought went into what they cut.

"Watch your god damn strokes," Patch screamed over the clash of steel and scuff of boots. Culp's blade sang bloody havoc as it sailed just over their heads, and for one mad moment, the warriors fought from their knees.

The shadow darted between their numbers, goading one to strike at another, which they did as often as at their foe.

As long as the blades danced, the shadow never missed another step. Five swords flashing in the dark, the moving pieces of the deadly game, each blade revealing its master's patterns. The shadow was beginning to enjoy the combat, and settled into the rhythm.

One, two, three, four, five.

One, two, three, four, five.

One, two, three, four ...

Four.

Someone had sat his turn, sheathed his blade; it was a cleverness the shadow had not considered possible in the townsmen. It was then that the demon realized it dealt with different sorts that night. It danced with warriors.

The shadow made to retreat, knowing it better to fight when it knew all the field. It did not like the game as much as when it played the other side.

The forceful arms that wrapped tightly around its waist had other ideas. Together, Sturmund and the shadow struck the floor.

"Cut its bloody head off, quickly," Hull stamped. "That's how you do for a witchy thing."

There was little in the way of disagreement. The puddling of blood trickling onto stone could be heard from many panting directions. None had gone unscathed, and the compliments wished to be returned.

To the dismay of both parties, Sturmund would not budge. Their Captain lay atop the pinned man— for it was, they all began to see in the accustomed dark, a man. Only Hull continued to doubt his eyes.

Sturmund held the pale figure down, dodging the teeth that snapped whenever tender throat came too near.

"You might fight like one," Sturmund said, his tone then unclear, "but you are no demon."

The figure only squirmed, falling limp on occasion, only to lull its possessor, before loosing another frantic burst.

"You are beaten," Sturmund said. "Yield."

At first, the figure did not reply, staring with odd calm at the rival atop him. Indeed, his strange presence seemed only to grow, for the greater the party's acclimation to the darkness, the more vibrant the shadow's eyes became. From their vantage, and despite present circumstances, Sturmund's men could not help but think the man not quite yet beaten.

"No." A single word, encompassing the whole of the downed man's being—defiance. Sturmund's eyes shone now as brightly as his captive's.

"It speaks," Patch said.

"From a forked tongue, no doubt," Hull added.

"Surrender yourself," Bitch said, stepping nearer the struggling figures. Something in the man's plight had spoken to her, the sight of him on his back, struggling vainly still, recalled for her another time. "And we will spare your life."

All heads but Sturmund's turned to the woman. The call had not been hers to make.

"The hell we will," Hull said, hefting up hammer to shoulder, inadvertently sending a spatter of blood, perhaps his own, onto the ground before him. The dark droplets stood rather nicely for his claim to the argument.

Even Patch, who usually cared little for what came at the end of a job, spoke against the man. He had found Bitch's conviction rather telling, and his spite drove him down the more sinister path. Even if he had no stake in a matter, Patch was never one to let another gain, when two could be made to suffer instead.

Culp stood by and watched, long blade resting on his shoulder, easily retrieved should his Captain call for it; just as easily sheathed should he not.

"I am not defeated," the pinned man said, as though perfectly at ease in the world. "A cornered fox is worth ten lazy hounds."

"My men are not lazy." Sturmund spoke to the insult. He would not suffer another to speak ill of his warriors, the weight of criticism he had placed earlier upon their backs meant only to strengthen.

"Their mouths told a different story." The gleaming eyes found Hull and held him, as much as the red warrior might wished to have looked away. "Loud, loud mouths."

"These loud mouths sent you running, paleskin" Patch said, thrusting the name out like a bodkin. "You turned tail when you heard us coming. Showed us just where to find your nest."

"I did not run. I simply came home." Their prisoner smiled sadly. "You would have come. Today. Tomorrow. It didn't matter, nor does it. Not anymore."

Sturmund, who knew what it was to have peace denied, thought he understood the sentiment.

"Why here?" their Captain asked, his hold never once loosening on the lean wrists, though the prisoner had been still for some time. "A man of your talents, you could have thrived in the poorest forest. Instead, you starve in one of the richest towns."

"She would not have survived it." Sturmund furrowed his brow, but the prisoner said no more. He simply lay.

Eyes wandered, searched; feet shuffled. At last, Bitch spoke.

"She did not survive."

Sturmund trusted in Bitch not to distract unless necessary. For the first time since pinning his prey, he turned his attention to matters elsewhere. In doing so, Sturmund knew, he had trusted in his prisoner as well.

The body was in the corner, so fragile and slight that Bitch dared not touch. She feared her rough hands might somehow further injure the delicate form. Instead, she simply bent beside it and studied the features.

She must have been a very old woman. The bones were wasted; the skin stretched over them, tight and thin. Bitch was a practiced eye for injuries; this creature had suffered.

"I told you. It does not matter anymore." The soft, high voice of their captive called Bitch back from her study. She had looked overlong, and felt sorry for the intrusion. She risked a touch, and tugged the woman's tattered cloak to better cover her modesty.

"She was your mother?" Bitch asked, another strange note catching Patch's ear.

Sturmund's grip had loosened; the man shrugged. "Perhaps. What is a mother? I only know that this one was kind to me."

"Why did you not bring her a doctor?" Culp looked distressed. The room had taken on the air of a tomb, and he wished to be gone from it.

"No one would have come to help. They shunned her. I do not know why." He cast a look at the body, but none of them understood what they saw in his eyes. "We found each other here. I fed her, bathed her. I shared the hours with her, tried to fight back the emptiness she said was eating at her. She claimed it was waiting for her to close her eyes, so I watched over her while she slept. But that is done now."

"They are not good people here." Culp spoke as though he might go and burn down the town.

"No, they are not." Bitch said, in a voice that suggested they might need to burn down the whole world.

"You are a fine blade." Their Captain's words were unexpected and drew silence from their crew, for they better than any knew the only two outcomes of such compliment. Either Sturmund would seek to test the true extent of his opponent's skill—a contest only one would survive—or this odd, pale man was to be offered a place among their own number—an honor, as they all had come to understand, that none was meant to survive.

"What do we call you?" Sturmund released his hold and stood, but did not help the man stand.

Rising silently to his feet, the paleskin shrugged in what was quickly becoming habit. "It does not matter how I am called today; only how I am remembered tomorrow."

Sturmund's eyes gleamed at the grand sentiment. "You have a place among us, if you like."

No one breathed. Silence dragged on. The darkness floated around them. And finally, the shoulders shrugged once more.

Sturmund clapped him on the arm, and it was done.

Patch groaned, while Hull visibly blanched, an irony that set Patch immediately back to humor.

"Do we bury your friend?" Bitch asked, almost as an afterthought as they were leaving the room. Death was never far from their minds, but they did not let it dwell in their hearts.

"She would not care," he said, not looking back. "That is no longer her."

"Well spoken," Sturmund said. "Back to the inn, now. You will take your oath, and we will sit beneath the moon, and you will tell me how you move so softly."

So saying, Sturmund strode away as though the melee were just a memory.

The rest followed suit, Hull pulling hesitantly alongside their new man.

"You . . . you always look like that?" Hull asked, never

taking his eyes from the skin, never coming close to meeting the brilliant gaze.

The paleskin cocked his head.

"I mean . . . it isn't witchery? You can't just change back?"

Bitch sighed.

"I meant no offense," Hull said, puffing his chest. "I just thought . . . something a bit more pleasing to the eye, was all, eh?"

And in an act either of mad generosity or desperate self-deception, Hull gave a friendly heave of his shoulder to the one he would later brand Ghost—or, he tried to, anyway. The shoulder never quite found its mark, Bitch smiling quietly at the rear as she watched the lithe figure bend away from the drifting ship. Hull staggered in the unexpected absence of support.

Patch cackled and slapped the old warrior on the back. "You really are dumb as an ox."

Hull reddened, sputtered, watching the pale man sail on ahead. "No, no . . ." He floundered as usual with the return. "Hung like one though."

Patch and Hull shared the cackle, their ugly music filling an uglier night. Sturmund had no more words for his men; his day had come to a satisfactory close. He gave only a nod to Culp, who grinned and set off to kill the alderman.

Ghost floated amongst them as they went, never settling, always drifting between or behind. In such uncommon company, it was easy to fall out of step.

"Come walk by me." The voice, still unpleasant, had lost something of its sharper edge in the skirmishes of the evening.

The pale man lingered and drew alongside her. Patch turned his head, good eye glancing back at the pair, and sneered.

The group walked on into the evening, their peculiar confederacy swelled by one.

~

"Patch?"

"Yes, Culp? I thought you had gone."

"I remembered something and had to come back."

"Well, what is it?"

"Don't ever call me a delicate flower again."

"What? When did I say that?"

"Earlier this evening. You thought I did not hear. But I did."

"Oh." Patch said, scarcely recalling the insult, but thinking it rather fitting; he did not repent. "Well, then maybe you should try not being such a del—"

Hull cackled; Bitch merely smirked.

A long-awaited smack was finally had, and all was right with the world that night.

6

Sturmund sat by the edge of the cliff and had watched impassively as the broad swath of sky darkened from its haze of white to an ever-deepening gray, until finally an ashen gloom settled like a pall over the hilltop. The men had set up the tents, but Sturmund never slept under cover if he could avoid it. He was a child of the old ways.

Hardship was to Sturmund mother's milk, the cold ground all the bed he had ever asked for. Even then, as a light rain began to fall, he thought the icy touch as pleasant as a woman's caress. His men did not share in his opinion, and sat wrapped in ragged blankets, no doubt weighing the benefit of leaky tent roofs against a dying fire.

An open sky above and the ground firmly beneath him, Sturmund had sat searching for clarity that evening. And what he sought, he had not found, his meditations bringing him only on to further doubt.

The days of glory seemed now behind him, the battles he had fought in youth long past. The wars of clans and kings, of skill and cunning, had been replaced by mindless skirmish, blind struggle in a sunken earth. He would not find his death in such brutish travail. Not the death he deserved. If he could have no death in glorious battle, he could have no death at all. And a life without end was a life without meaning. Sturmund could think of nothing worse.

The rain quickened, pelting indifferently against his scalp and face, relentless in its single-minded assault. Sturmund's chest tightened, his blood rising under the stress of long days, the violence of his hands always a single thought from true expression. But he was master there, the man alone—neither the world with its petty abuse, nor the soul in its melancholic inclination, should ever prove otherwise.

The pressure inside of him grew.

The great man could have loosed a cry to split the sky and call down the thunder. He had, in his time, turned back tides of soldiers with such a bellow, stunned armies with the force of his voice alone. But Sturmund did not call out. Sturmund was a warrior. There were no foes to face on that cliff, only a tired man to be brought to his senses. A weary sigh followed as he allowed himself to fall to a trance deeper still, the worry and the uncertainty shedding like so much dross soon after. Then, there was only the night.

There was a hush of grass under delicate foot, so smooth and soft that Sturmund had almost missed her approach entirely. But almost was, for that night, good enough, and he released his grip of the sword hilt on his lap.

"Come and sit by me." Sturmund's voice was concealed in part by the falling of the rain, but Bitch had ears that missed nothing.

She walked closer, emerging from the shadows as though parting a veil, stepping into his view from behind a curtain of night.

"What is it you see when you look out there?" When she

spoke to Sturmund, she spoke tenderly—or as tenderly as her nature allowed.

"I see nothing. I see clouds before my eyes." Sturmund sat cross-legged, the length of his blade resting across his thighs. He made no attempt to wipe the rain as it ran down his face, into his eyes, along the strands of pale-blond hair.

"And what is it you hope to see?" She was next to him now, close to him, sharing the ground and the night, his company and perhaps his confidence, but nothing more. "What is at the end of it all?"

"There is nothing at the end," Sturmund said, his tone tranquil, almost reverent, "except the end. That is a beautiful thing."

"What if there were more?" Not even the falling rain and empty sky could hide the hope in the woman's voice.

Sturmund's eyes held the dark horizon, where a black sea met a blacker sky, and Bitch, who even then enjoyed the warmth of his body next to hers, knew he was no longer with her.

As they sat, each in their silence, she eyed with resentment the sword cradled on his lap, the calloused hands tender where they rested on the lifeless metal. The ache inside her grew, and she pretended it was not there, hiding it amongst the many other pains, lost with all the rest. She never resented the man, only the warrior within. She tried to enjoy the moment anyway.

"Hull and Ghost should have returned by now." In Sturmund's words came an order, and Bitch, with a look to the sky for the hour, knew he was correct.

"I will go," she answered, already on her feet, taking her leave gratefully.

"Take Patch."

There was a sudden scuff as her sure strides faltered in

the dark. If she wished to protest, she did not, knowing her Captain was correct.

Sturmund had a way of seeing and knowing that the others did not. That was, in part, why he was their Captain. He found the weak links and reforged them. Culp and Patch's spat was through, Bitch and Patch's only beginning. Sturmund knew this, and in sending the two out into the night, was rethreading the weakness, bringing together that which time always sought to tear asunder. Sturmund knew this, and now so did Bitch.

She walked off stinging from the knowledge.

7

Hull was running—sometimes on two legs, limping badly with each step; sometimes on all fours, grunting and disheveled, a harried fox desperate for a hole.

Ghost was gone; Hull believed him dead. He did not dwell on it: dead was dead. Their kind was no stranger to bad ends. Hull only wished he could get the screaming out of his ears, but just then something even worse pursued him.

A wail sounded in the distance that froze Hull dead before setting him to an ever more urgent climb of the slope. He grabbed the hateful vines, grasping sharp leaves that cut his hands, and dug deeply into the cold earth for stronger roots to hold. He used the plants for leverage, anchors to help him up the incline. He slipped twice, slid down a slickness of mud, before reaching the top, exhausted.

The wailing sounded again, closer. Hull turned.

Thunder pealed, a deafening crack that lingered in the air, rolling through the forest and over Hull. Then came more lightning, and in that phantom glow Hull saw what was coming for him, through the trees and the mud, closer every moment, hungry for his flesh.

Hull ran.

8

"They probably got lost. I've known Hull to lose his way in his own tent." Patch tried to cut some of the tension. His mood was fouler than usual, but he had no wish for another confrontation that night.

"Ghost doesn't get lost." They were the only words Bitch had spoken since they had set out. She had no desire to speak with Patch, but would not let him cast aspersions on a man as competent as Ghost. She knew what it was to be thought less of for being different through no fault of one's own, and owing to some kindred spark shared with the paleskin, she spoke on his behalf. Besides, Sturmund had wished her and Patch to mend their differences. She would try—for him.

"I suppose he doesn't. It would be pretty hard to, at least, glowing as he does." Patch's laugh was ugly to Bitch's ears. He was, to her, more child than man. That would not spare him a beating if he persisted. She pressed on ahead of him, placing him out of sight, if not out of mind; his incessant nattering made such a feat impossible.

Patch didn't mind following behind a woman. He was a

better tracker by far, but she was doing well enough. He rather enjoyed the features of Bitch's hindquarters. From his angle, she almost looked like a real woman, not the feral thing he knew her to be. Still, he wouldn't say no to a roll with her—so long as she promised not to bite his prick off.

Bitch felt the hungry eyes on her, leering at her legs, lusting for her to submit. It calmed her some. She relished the power she had. No matter how often she taught the lesson, a new student seemed always at hand. Patch hovered dangerously close to becoming one of her pupils.

"There," Bitch said, finally picking up the trail that Patch had spotted half a mile back. She bent low to examine the tracks.

"Nice work, girl. Found 'em at last." He picked with care the voice best suited to rankle and had settled upon one appropriately patronizing. He had no intention of sticking it in Bitch when it was much more fun to stick it to her.

The rain had not relented. It had been coming down for the past hour, still a drizzle, not enough to obscure the tracks, nowhere near enough to force them back. It was odd, though, that Hull and Ghost had not returned and that they had not met them on the trail. Ghost was wiser than to stay out in bad weather, and Hull hated the rain for how it aged him; his bloody locks would not stand washing. It all boded poorly, and Bitch and Patch both found themselves frequently patting their weapons the further on they trekked.

"That's their tracks out," Patch said, coming alongside. He pointed to the barely perceptible treads, the hide-wrapped boots Ghost wore that let him move so softly. "Ghost went ahead, Hull followed after some time."

Bitch had no trouble making out the deep depressions,

even then filling with rain and leaves, that Hull's heavy feet had left behind—in truth, more crater than footprint.

"There's nothing coming back," Patch said, looking around to see if they might have taken a different route back towards camp. "They're still out there."

Patch and Bitch both looked into the distance, their eyes following the direction of the tracks. They looked at one another, and Bitch could see the apprehension beneath Patch's easy smile. Bitch nodded.

They drew their weapons and picked up their pace.

9

When he opened his eyes, he saw nothing—no trees, no sky, only blackness, emptiness. And were it not for the agony wrenching at his lungs, the fire searing in his chest, Ghost would have thought himself dead. Instead, he found his face caked with mud, sludge like tar, heavy, suffocating.

With frantic, clawing hands, he raked the muck from his eyes, from his mouth, blew the filth from his nostrils and gagged at the clods of stale earth caught in his throat. Had he known what rank odor was then to assail him, he might have reconsidered, might have let himself drown in the slopping folds of the mire. As it was, there remained nothing to dampen the rot and stink, and Ghost thought he might go blind from the obscenity of it all.

He turned his head to the side and vomited out blackness, emptying the entire contents of his stomach. He had not eaten since the day before. Only earth and bile fell from his mouth.

The cave was drowned in shadow thick as the slop and vomit he lay in. What light seeped through the cracks in the stone roof shone only faintly into the tunnels. Violet eyes gleamed in the dark as Ghost took in what little there was to see.

He was alone, a fact that should have brought him some relief. Whatever it was that had set upon them in the woods was not with him then, but neither was his companion. That would not do.

Ghost could remember little enough, his head still clouded with delirious pain, but what he did recall troubled him deeply—tooth and fang, claw and muscle. He shuddered with the memory, and then shamed with it. He had not heard the creature approach, had not even sensed it stalking them. And that was bad. If he had not been equal to it, there stood little chance the others would be prepared either. He needed to get to them, and quickly.

He strained to sit up, and immediately the pain ripped through his body—nerves on fire, flesh opening, muscles spasming. There was blind noise and shocking color in his mind. It was as if his entire body were screaming. He dropped back onto the sodden earth. Then came the blood.

What little mending and clotting the wound had managed in the time he had been unconscious had been undone in one foolish moment. He examined the mess with great care, lifting his head and craning his neck as far as the torn flesh of his stomach would allow.

He could see the tear in his shirt, the dark-sodden fabric surrounding the wound. Carefully, very carefully, he raised the shirt, the stinging tug of flesh adhering to the garment slowing his progress.

His stomach churned when he saw the wound. It was deep, and it was wide. His abdomen looked a ruin, and the flesh puckered and sucked where teeth and claws had sunk deepest, the blood welling dark, hot, black. The great, unknown something had dragged him in its mouth.

Waves of nausea rolled through Ghost's stomach, and with their ebb came only exhaustion. He lay on the wet earth for some time, not moving, merely dying. The pain was nothing new to him; his collection of scars and hurt was as expansive as any of their lot. What cut him more deeply than claw or fang was the certain knowledge that he had a choice: rise or fall; suffer or rest; live or die. The difference, Ghost knew, between a mortal wound and a good story to tell by the firelight came down to a simple matter of will. At that most grievous moment, alone and soiled, Ghost despaired, because he knew his mind.

He closed his eyes.

The silence of the cave drew closer; the shadows followed. The motionless figure welcomed them, and the wasted moments ran on. For blissful minutes, nothing stirred.

You linger.

Ghost's eyes opened. There was no fear, nor, if he considered carefully, any surprise. In the blue darkness of the caverns, Sturmund sat watching from the shadows.

"I—"

You. The word carried with it not just the sober timbre of his Captain's voice, but the crushing weight of accusation. *Can you breathe?*

"I am dying."

Every night we die. Every morning we live again.

"I am tired." The pleading tone sounded almost childish in the emptiness of the cave.

From the shadows, the breathing rose and fell, slow and deep, patient and unmoved. Ghost could see the figure, but little of the face, bathed as it was in fulsome shadows. The presence, however, was undeniable.

"I will bleed out."

Not yet. The blue eyes gleamed in the gloom, piercing the shadows, pinioning Ghost with their intensity. Under their weight, he knew himself lacking. *Not before you pay back the courtesy to the one who has done this. Only then do you have my leave.*

A smile came to Ghost's lips, the dry skin splitting with the movement. Ghost had never known Sturmund to say a thing that was not so, and thus resigned himself to live, if only that he might better die.

"Yes, my Captain." And with that, the warrior set to his task.

He had little on his person, his pack gone, lost to the wilderness. A single satchel remained to him, tied to the waist of his trousers, and with its sparse contents he did what he could. The hide he found was not clean, nor did it hug the skin nearly tight enough to staunch the flow of blood. But it was all he had, and so it sufficed.

Hurry, my warrior. Sturmund's voice was fading, and Ghost looked up to find him gone from his seat, his presence distant, though his voice lingering still. *Your death is still out there, waiting.*

"Captain," Ghost called, remembering himself and his charge, "it is coming for the camp. A beast. It has our scent. It will sniff you out."

A soft laughter sounded in the dark, but the owner had gone. Still, the voice echoed all around in the empty halls of stone.

Then pity the beast.

Ghost thought on the words and the man who had spoken them; they were a part of him, in his bones.

We Burn Our Dead

As Ghost fled the cave, wending his way unsteadily through the dark, he stumbled, first on bones, a graveyard of every conceivable type of death beneath his feet. There were bones of elk and deer, boar and fox, wolf and wildcat. Ghost recognized them all on sight. There were new bones, stained with rotting sinew and caked with stale blood, left to molder on the cavern floor. There were old bones, blanched by air and time, stripped clean and calcified into solid stone. There was all this, and there was more, for as Ghost pushed himself to his feet, his hands slid deeper into the rotting pile, his arms almost to the elbow by the time his hands touched the earth below.

He made to stand and stumbled again, landing hard in the heap and displacing some of the lighter debris with the weight of his body.

Then he saw the heavier bones, the human bones that lay beneath, the thick thigh bones of men, the rib cages and pelvises of both sexes, the skulls of old and young alike. And at the bottom of the heap, beneath piles of death and rot, something bright and shining.

Ghost's eyes widened, and he forgot for a moment his pain and the danger of his companions. His violet eyes saw only gold.

10

Sturmund had finally surrendered his quest for enlightenment. The night would not talk to him, nor had his inner voice anything to offer his troubled soul. He went to join the others by the fire.

Culp was exactly where he had been all night, resting by his pack, giving no mind to the light rain falling on his head. Sturmund nodded his approval.

Marney had chosen a different approach, one more cautious and fastidious as befitted his character. He sat beneath a makeshift canopy, fashioned from his spare cloak, legs folded beneath him as he scanned the pages of a book, taking care not to let any rain stain its parchment or run its ink.

The grizzled scholar brushed a hand over the corner of one page, wiping away a stray droplet. He turned his pale eyes to the sky and scowled. Any harder and he would have to move inside.

Most times, rain was the warrior's friend. Sturmund's troops worked well in the muck, had been trained by their Captain to use it to their advantage. Their company had steady feet and good balance, and knew how best to tread a sodden field. Many were the times Sturmund had delayed their advance, his hawkish eyes watching the sky, conferring with Marney over the likelihood of bad weather. When they marched it was with the storms and the clouds, when not even Death could grasp their mud-slicked bodies.

Most times, rain was their friend—but on nights such as these, it served only to inconvenience, to intrude upon their precious restful hours, to drive them from the fire and into the shabby discomfort of their leaky shelters. They preferred to be out of doors where a man could breathe, and where death could be seen well ahead of its approach.

"Cap'n," Marney said, nodding respectfully to his old friend. Culp echoed the sentiment.

"What do you read tonight, Scholar?" Sturmund's voice was solemn and weighty, no different than any other time he spoke.

"A history of the kings," Marney said, his voice dry and brittle. "I've read it before."

"Have you nothing better to read, then?"

Marney sighed.

"I've read them all," he said, nodding behind him towards the mouth of his tent where sat the scholar's heavy pack, insides bursting with scroll and text, a ponderous cargo that the hard old soldier would trust no other to haul up and down the uncertain countryside.

"Time we got you some new material." Sturmund eyed the pack. "If you think your old bones are up to it."

Marney grinned. "You just look to your own load. You travel light for a warrior. A sword and a tent? Where's the training in that? Pretty soon you won't be able to lift that steel."

"That day comes for us all." Sturmund spoke almost

wistfully, and Marney realized he had turned the Captain onto a favorite theme. "But you are right, Scholar, we all need to challenge ourselves if we are to be ready for the end. I travel with nothing because I deny myself everything. You travel with the weight of knowledge crushing down upon you. We both train well, I think."

Marney studied the Captain, standing so immovably in the cold and the rain, looking like a man always alone, no matter where he was. He searched for the words that might bring comfort to his friend, but for all his learning, found himself unequal to the task. Still, he wished to try, but just before mouth could give voice to thought, the night interceded and set them all on a different course.

Something distant, something faint, carried on the wind, a whisper—the ghost of a sound, the sound of a ghost. Sturmund and Marney and Culp all looked towards the treeline. Across the narrow road from their camp, the forest stood bathed in heavy shadow.

Thunder cracked and the sky lit above them, the rough shapes of wraith-like clouds momentarily visible to them below. The rain fell harder—Sturmund did not seem to notice, Marney began to gather his things, Culp drew a hood over his head.

"Do you have a map of these lands?"

"You know I do," Marney said. "We studied it long hours together before . . . the previous engagement." Marney hated himself for giving new life to that shameful battle.

Sturmund said nothing, nodding slowly. He appeared distracted, an odd tension to his looks, as though his head wished to turn away, towards the woods perhaps, if only his muscles would allow it. But Sturmund's body, like his mind, did nothing Sturmund did not wish it to.

Marney sensed the unease and, like a catching fever, it jumped quickly to the old scholar.

"Shall I fetch them out?" Marney rose to his knees and began to forage through his pack.

"Bring them to my tent when you have them," Sturmund said, turning. "I fear I may have made a mistake."

Culp looked up at this, but unable to make much of the comment and never one to pursue a difficult thought, returned to cleaning his nails with a dagger he had lifted from Patch's pack.

11

Bitch froze. The cry came faint and distant to her ear, muddled by the patter of rain, subdued by the yawning of the wind, but still she had heard.

Patch listened, also. They had spread out following the trail of their companions, casting a wide net of their search so as not to miss returning tracks. They did not wish to venture out blindly forever when the possibility existed, however remote, that Hull and Ghost had taken a different path back to camp.

At the cry, the two had drawn together on the trail, such as it was. The path was sodden dirt slightly more beaten than what lay around them, but so overgrown with brush that it scarcely qualified as anything more than a guess.

It had been Patch who drew nearer his fellow tracker, her presence an unlikely comfort. At the second sounding of the same wretched call, Bitch realized her own gratitude at not being alone in so dismal a place.

"Can you make it out?" Bitch asked, softly as she could. Her deference to his skill spoke volumes on their situation.

Patch stood almost shoulder-to-shoulder with her now,

their legs ankle deep in mud and sinking with every step. He shook his head in answer, then shook it again to clear the rain and strands of sodden hair from his eye.

"Can't tell. Might be a bear," he said, his eye squinting in the direction from which they both seemed to have agreed the sound had come. "Might not be."

The mud alone, sucking hungrily at their feet, could not explain the difficulty Bitch had in urging herself onward. Were it not for the perpetual ease of Patch's air, even there in that mire, in those blighted woods, she thought she might have remained frozen forever, rooted to the spot until she perished, another grisly feature amongst the rotting trees.

"Come on, girl," Patch said, turning back to his motionless companion, one corner of his mouth rising in a wry grin. "I'll show you the way."

She could have cut him for that. Part of her would always wish she had. But she trudged on, wrenching her foot from the slurping mess, focusing on the miles ahead.

12

"It goes on for miles," Marney said, leaning over the map. The scholar had unfurled the parchment upon the ground of Sturmund's empty tent, and together they plotted their position, traced their straggling path from village to ruined village to their present point at the top of the seaside cliffs.

Sturmund squinted over the penciled borders, the faint coloring of mountain and town and water that filled the busy chart. Above all, he studied the woods, noting how small the squares of green appeared on the whole of the parchment. Then he consulted the scale and furrowed his brow.

They were none of them overly familiar with the lands they had come to, though all their homes and haunts lay somewhere within the same great borders as held the sprawling forest. The kingdom was vast, and only Hull and Sturmund had ever ventured beyond its limits—but that was a lifetime ago, when both had taken to the seas, Hull for fortune, Sturmund for the toil. Both had found only death, and, eventually, each other.

Marney tapped a thin finger onto the patch of pale green, someway past the grey line that indicated the road, practically a strand of hair upon unwieldy parchment. "That's as far as they could have gone."

The scholar fished a nub of charcoal from his pocket and traced two arcing lines from the point, each meeting the road some distance apart. "And with Hull along, I'd be surprised if they made it half as far."

Sturmund looked at the boundary Marney had drawn. It was scarcely any distance at all, and Sturmund knew his second was correct—they could not have wandered far. What worried him was how small a fraction of the forest lay within the penciled marking, and how immense a swath lay without. If his men had somehow gotten turned around and carried on past the arbitrary boundary, they would be at the mercy of the elements for at least the night.

"No sense fretting," Marney said, casually, "Ghost could never get himself lost."

There was a moment before Sturmund spoke, during which pregnant silence Marney realized his unflappable Captain had indeed begun to worry.

"That's my point, Scholar. They should have returned. And if they haven't, then something has befallen them."

Marney eyed the map more closely, wondering just what existed within the neat little grid that could actually pose a threat to such men as theirs. It did not seem likely any bandit would occupy so remote a place, nor did the terrain look to present much challenge with Ghost as guide.

"And I have sent two more," Sturmund said, interrupting Marney's study. "Two more into this unknown. I was not thinking clearly." Sturmund paused, and thought about the night and the rain and how willingly he had let himself be kept apart from his men. "I was distracted."

"They'll be back." Marney was not trying to convince the Captain. He truly believed the men would return, despite the knot that had begun tightening in his gut. Ghost and Hull, Bitch and Patch—they had each survived too much hardship and suffering to be brought low by a humble forest and some rain.

The sky lit up again, a brilliant flash that turned the walls of the tent white.

"I hope you are right," was all Sturmund said.

13

In the light of day, the forest by the sea appeared a lush and pleasant place, if a bit too uncertain for the casual traveler to explore. The ground stretched placidly from the treeline, sinking and rolling gracefully soon thereafter, and the thick spread of oaks and pine quickly narrowed until straightforward passage proved impossible, the hapless wanderer forced to weave between trunks so frequently that maintaining a sense of direction became a challenge, the sun and sky all but blotted out by the layers of canopy above.

That was during the day. At night, when only slivers of starlight and moonbeam cut to the forest floor, limning the silent horde of trees, travel became blind and desperate. Covering almost every spot of ground was the untamed diffusion of greenery, a most dense and unrelenting underbrush that existed seemingly only to trip up the wanderer and bring him down hard upon his stomach. If he were a lucky traveler, he might avoid as he fell the many sharp and solid stones concealed beneath the brush. If not, there were denizens of the forest aplenty who would be grateful for the meal.

And then there was the rain. It fell hard in the forest, cascading from on high, pooling along the canopy and thundering down upon the earth in heavy streams, beating and churning the floor into an endless and inescapable morass. The patter that came with the rain deafened, no sound existing but the slap of jagged drops against stone and leaf and dirt. Rivers were born where before lay only parched earth, rushing floodwaters trampling the low-lands, slipping into sudden chasms along the forest floor, drowning subterranean chambers and all life within.

It was into this untamed world that Sturmund's men had come, untroubled by what first they had seen. They had looked on the place undeterred and carried on, hard men who had faced far worse in their time than a bit of mud and rain.

It was not the rain that troubled them now; it was the nightmare—the lurking, hulking thing that slumbered in the forest depths, that woke to the sound of their heartbeats, that rose on staggering feet, stretching and shaking off the dust of long years. It was the teeth and tongue—sharp and wet, cutting and cruel—that frightened them. It was the eyes of blackest night, the skin impenetrable, the hunger insatiable. It was the hunt that made them run, the prey they had become.

And none of them knew which way was out.

14

Hull faded. The forest had taken his spirit and had sharp designs on everything else. The ruddy face was caked with earth, the white, terrified eyes standing out against the black filth. His braids had come undone, and his long hair, his proud red mane, lay washed of its strident color, pale straw on a scarecrow face.

He had fallen. He did not know from how high, nor for how long he had lain catching his breath, but he had fallen. The rain-slick forest would suffer none to tread its ground upright. It brought everything to its knees, and then its back.

The old warrior lay with his arms outstretched, palms pressed into the cold, wet earth, which felt to him like the mealy pulp of dead flesh. The rain beat mercilessly, carrying more silt into his eyes. The ground began to tremble.

Hull could feel it through his hands, all along his flattened, limp body: the thunder of hooves approaching, the tread of the immense.

Blindly, he reached for his hammer, but he had lost it in the fall. He had lost much in the fall.

The ground shook more fiercely so that the thick muscle

of his chest began to quake, the echo of the beating hooves resonating within, lashing at his heart. They were the footsteps of death, and they came on all fours.

Hull regretted nothing save his fear of the past hours. It had been a long life with very little to surrender to—a hard head and a hard heart had seen to that. But the shame he felt at having to quit his life, knowing he did so full of trepidation, filled him with a rage that forced him to his knees. A broken back would not stop a giant from rising, and the blood he coughed only gave him more to spit. Even on his knees, the old warrior made a formidable sight.

Hull found his hammer half-buried in the mire, the greedy earth no contender when it tried to keep it from him. He snatched free the weapon as easily as plucking a flower, held it tight, and raised it above his head. This time, the thunder above deferred to an old warrior's roar.

The earth quaked. The beast came crashing through trees, its head bending into moss-covered trunks, a shattering spray of splinters filling the air as it burst through the wood. It did not gallop, lacking as it did any manner of grace, but on wild, furious hooves it threw itself along the forest floor.

The old warrior no longer doubted that what came for him then had been coming for him all his life.

Hull took careful aim, knowing his end was near, that his last act must do much to redeem all the rest.

He smiled at the beast, and welcomed him home; he laughed at the brute, and showed him his teeth. And shaking what little remained of his bloody locks, loosed a thunderous cry and sent his hammer sailing.

It was a practiced throw, a master's throw, and when Hull finally perished, an art that would go with him to the grave. But the beast would not be turned away by the impudence of a single blow, and Hull knew even then that the iron bulk of his storied hammer, moving perfectly through the air, would not be enough. The beast came on.

Hull did not take his eyes from his cast, satisfied with his effort, his powerful lungs still bellowing, the creature's face so terribly near. And as the hammer struck, the smack of stolid iron against chillingly thick bone, so too did the arrows, so too did the knives.

Hull was a broad man, stalwart and brave. Grown men trembled in his shadow. That same girth proved most challenging to Bitch and Patch, who took aim from some remove, their line of sight all but obscured by the old warrior's massive frame.

The arrows flew straight and true, fluffing Hull's paled hair as they whizzed over one shoulder. Patch did not wait to see if they landed before stringing another volley.

Bitch's bolt came across Hull's other shoulder, faster and angrier than any arrow ever could, and even as the twang of bowstring rang out, she had dropped the crossbow and chanced a throw with her knives, rushing towards her fallen comrade as she did.

The hammer had not been enough. The beast who had walked through trees shrugged off the blow like water. The arrows, the bolt, the blades—they turned tides and beast both, the hulking mass of bone and gnashing teeth diverting its course before it could put Hull beneath its hoof.

They did not wait for the beast to regroup. As the creature roared its displeasure, running feverous in the distance, scraping its face to the earth as it tried to dislodge sharp steel from its hateful eye, the two trackers took hold of their lost warrior and proceeded to drag him from the forest.

They heaved mightily—arms hooked under the old warrior's shoulders, Hull hauled backwards and on his broad backside—but once they overcame the initial drag, steady momentum eased them into their work.

Patch and Bitch were by far the slenderest of their company, Hull by far the most unwieldy. It did not help, as they each wrapped an arm around the tree-like limbs, that the old warrior kept hurling invective towards the direction of the stomping, baying shadows.

"That's right, you nasty beastie," Hull yelled. "There's plenty more of that to be had."

"Shut up, you old fool," Patch spat, tugging at him harder.

Bitch remained silent, focusing on their already impossible task without bothering to take on yet another. When the old warrior set himself to quarrel, no measure of coaxing had ever been proven to quiet him.

"And I'll be coming back fer my hammer..."

Hull went, laughing, his booming voice slowly receding into one direction as the seething howls of the slighted creature moved off in another.

15

The satchel was heavy. Ghost had taken what he could, two blind fistfuls stuffed greedily into the leather bag. There was enough for all of them, a way to keep warm through the coming cold, enough to catch their breath, but as he stumbled, vision blurring, mind slipping towards the dark, he began to doubt they would any of them ever spend a single coin.

A cry sounded in the distance, the calls of more than beast, the shouts of men and steel clashing in the night. Ghost struggled to keep upright, his talented ears and hunter's eye showing him two paths—one towards the safety of camp, the other the way of the struggle, where his companions labored even then against the beast.

Ghost smarted at the thought of that fell creature. He and Hull had been so thoroughly waylaid, all the more improbably for the great mass of the beast that had descended upon them. All had been still, the fires of camp a distant but pleasant lure. They had been hastening through the rain, their arms laden with trophies for the spit, Hull humming a low tune of war and women as they went.

Then violence. Noise. Anguish.

It had come upon them from the trees, *through* the trees. Ghost recalled the sting of shrapnel, shivered wood and jagged splinters, long as claws and twice as sharp, lashing his face.

Hull had struck first, hammer following fist, a mighty warrior so easily repulsed.

Ghost recalled his own part, how he had made to strike from below, lunging towards the creature's flank, aiming for the soft flesh of its underbelly—but there was no soft flesh, and there was no surprise.

In a single moment, both men had fallen—Hull dispatched to the dark, his head having finally found something harder than his own skull; Ghost to a world of pain, helpless beneath trampling claws, dragged off to the larder of an impossible beast.

It had meant to shred his flesh, to tear from bone all that was tender and meaty, and it would have succeeded, or rather, finished, had Hull not sought them out. Such powerful lungs on that ginger-headed brute, calling, taunting, challenging the beast to follow as he fled the mouth of its lair. Such mad heroics to lure away certain death for the sake of a dying comrade.

Ghost turned his ear to the wind, the faint snatches of Hull's booming voice thin and powerless by the time it reached him, the sharp growl of the beast not one degree softened. Battle raged in the distance, and Ghost knew already what must be the fatal result.

Violet eyes looked once more towards the path to camp and the dream of safety at its end, the heavy satchel and his aching side both tugging him that way.

Ghost looked to the path and then ran the other way.

16

There had been nothing but night all the way, an appallingly thick and clinging blackness that poured into their eyes and mouths, blinding, suffocating. Behind them was the beast, somewhere in the darkness it called home. It had bayed and growled, whined and howled from the shadows, but for whatever reason had remained out of sight, always following, always near.

They were going to die, that much seemed clear to them as they raced through the forest, the snarling beast any moment to descend upon them, its amusement with the chase overcome at last by mindless hunger. They would die in the rain and the mud. Bitch thought it as fine a place as any.

Hull had fallen silent, his heavy body slack, his tremendous head slumped and bobbing against his chest as they dragged him over the wet, uneven ground. He would not know it when death came to take him. Bitch knew that would have upset the old warrior, and she hoped he would wake before the end, if only for a glimpse.

Their breath tore raggedly from their throats, coming

fast and desperate, their lungs burned by exhaustion and the chill air. Patch had begun to cough, a constant hacking, painful and grating. Bitch sounded no better. And had the lights of camp not suddenly appeared in the black distance ahead, they surely would have succumbed to their exhaustion and their deaths, carrion for the beast to collect. Their eyes could scarcely believe.

"Ho!" Patch cried, sounding nothing like himself, the graveled, throaty tones frightful to Bitch's ears. He was gasping with the effort, coughing at the rain that caught in his throat, tripping over his feet from the exertion.

There was a scrape of unsheathed steel and the murmur of distant voices from outside the treeline, a few fleeting shadows crossing in front of the glowing firelight.

"Who comes?" a voice called. Bitch would know Culp anywhere by his eager and sturdy tones. She sighed her relief, never once slackening her pace.

"Your comrades," Bitch called out. "Pursued," she added, somehow finding the breath to get the word across.

"Then come fast," another voice said, "and let us be your shield."

Bitch felt her eyes wet with more than rain. Sturmund's sure command, impossible to resist, overwhelmed.

They stumbled into camp, their skin torn and bleeding from the snatching branches, lungs bursting, bodies failing. They carried Hull out of the brush and did not stop until they were safely behind the line of men that had risen to their defense.

Sturmund and Culp stood at the fore, facing the silent treeline, swords readied, spirits steeled. Even old Marney had taken up his spear, so firm and steady in his hands that Bitch saw in him nothing of the scholar and everything of the man. And for one mad moment, she actually wished the beast would come. Let it slip its cowardly cover and enter the open field. She would like nothing better than for it to meet her companions.

Hull lay senseless on the sodden ground, as Patch strung his bow with unsteady hands. Bitch quelled her nausea enough to raise blades of her own. The warriors stood silent in the rain, minds hard as steel, focused only on the coming battle.

They waited.

And waited.

No such battle came.

Culp gripped and regripped his sword hilt, blinking away rain and spitting. Sturmund was as a statue, immovable and grave, his sword point never wavering.

Still, nothing.

Bitch had regained some manner of composure, her breath still deep and heavy, and she thought about warning Sturmund of what was coming. If only she could find the words.

The night answered on her behalf.

An awful cracking, long, slow, like tendons of a waking giant, filled the shadows of the forest. An earth-shattering crash followed, and it shook more than earth.

Patch staggered back a pace, even Culp flexing his arms a little tighter.

Bitch knew the sound. It had pursued them all through the night, the footsteps of a monster, the crush of trunks beneath its weight.

More trees fell, a series of rolling crashes, brutish commotion brought by the wrathful advance of the beast. It neared, pines, even oak, swaying, and the shadows beyond began to thicken as something filled the blackness with a presence darker still.

Everything stopped. Silence fell.

A looming phantom stared out at them from the darkness of the treeline. Another step would take it into range of the campfire, but the beast remained within its shroud, veiled by shadow, the thin curtain of night all that held back the madness of battle.

Five warriors stood before the mouth of the forest, and all looked into that darkness, straining to see, needing to understand.

It was Sturmund who looked deepest, and as he did, the shadows shifted, the creature within turning slowly its unseen gaze. As the eyes of the beast passed over their number, each warrior let out a shiver, a wave of revulsion filling them in turn, all except lonely Sturmund, upon whom the gaze fell and finally settled.

What Sturmund saw in that lightless void, none would ever ask, nor would their Captain ever say. But what they glimpsed in Sturmund's eyes when he turned to them later that night offered more than any wished to know.

It would seem to Marney, who knew his Captain best, or as well as any man who fought beside another could, that some of the shadows had come away with him, pulled from the forest depths like corrupted cotton, clinging to his eyes and lashes, in his sight and on his mind from that moment on. It troubled the scholar, who would find himself looking away whenever Sturmund chanced too near. He would turn to his books for his answers, knowing they held no such miracles.

And from that singular stillness in which the warriors were locked, a silence from which none of them thought they would ever escape, never again to hear the songs of birds or clash of steel, came a noise greater than anything their number had ever faced, a bellowing so loud and fierce that a return to quiet seemed impossible, the world forever drowned in the fury of that cry.

It erupted from nothingness, shaking trees and earth, sending leaves bristling and whipping on their branches. The wind that came from within those forest depths carried with it the stench of death, not only of flesh, but of time, for this creature was the eater of worlds, the devourer of souls.

Culp blanched, and Marney dropped his arms, the polished spear tip slipping into the earth before him. Hull let out a whimper from the darkness in which he lay wrapped, the endless roar having pursued him even there, and Bitch looked on him and what the creature had made of such a proud warrior. She slipped to her knees, and placed a comfortless hand upon his breast. The heartbeat below her fingers raced.

Then it was over.

The noise ended, in time, as all things surely must.

They none of them spoke right away.

The beast had lumbered off, the earth shaking, trembling, then merely rumbling, as the great form loped back into the dark heart of the forest.

Sturmund turned to look at Patch and Bitch and battered Hull. He did not know who to ask, or how. His eyes spoke the question he found he could not form, as though the creature, when it had stolen off, had taken with it his voice.

Patch looked at Sturmund with a blank expression, the eternal grin at last wiped clean.

"There's a monster in those woods," was all Patch said.

Sturmund nodded his agreement.

17

Hull was delirious, his back broken in three places Marney told them, and Bitch thought back to the sight of the crippled warrior clambering to his knees. There was no explanation for that in any of the scholar's books of medicine, only in the tomes of the heroes were such feats recorded.

What Hull reported to them of Ghost and the beast came fragmented and strange. The old warrior's sobs embarrassed them; his sudden spasms of pain chastened them.

They listened to his rambling oaths, his feverish vows of revenge. What he had to say of Ghost disheartened them. There seemed little chance their brother had survived, or, if he had, would be likely to make it through the remainder of the stormy evening.

Hull demanded to be dragged back to the place of battle, where he could reclaim his victory, restore his injured pride. Some great, aching part of him sought to bring home the man he had left behind—whether that man was Ghost or the red warrior himself was a matter of much inward debate around the fire that evening.

All knew Hull had acted properly. None thought the old warrior a coward, nor believed he had fled. Still, when two men set out together, it is shameful for only one to return.

When he called for his hammer and made to rise, wincing and collapsing back onto the blanket, Marney had to tell him of its loss. The broken warrior raved and raged at the only thing in his line of sight, a wolfish moon, yellow and leering, and towards its lofty heights, he hurled his fury.

Hull soon settled into angry silence, a throbbing, brooding wrath that told them all it was time to leave him be. Marney had done what little he could to ease the discomfort of his broken body. Only rest and time might see him well. Alas, there was nothing in the scholar's kit for use on a wounded pride.

Those that remained sat round the fire together, a broken circle silently watching the blazing wood. They could not bring themselves to look upon one another, so each stared into the flames, and there, at least, their hearts and minds found common ground.

In the morning, they would go and seek their missing man.

18

Night clung with greedy hands. Daybreak lay a ways off yet, and the weight of the brooding darkness made all doubt if morning might ever come.

Something came, if not the dawn.

Sturmund reacted first, his sword escaping its sheath even before the others could stand. Culp and Bitch were not far behind, with Patch and Marney taking up the rear—Marney preparing to issue tactical commands, Patch simply happy to let someone else fall on the first sword while he finished stringing his bow.

It approached from the trees, moving fast, too fast, clumsily even. No sane man would attack an encampment in so careless a fashion. Only a beast had such a mind.

Sturmund raised his sword into a high guard, preparing to defend against a violent blow, ready to respond in kind.

Their Captain seemed somehow larger to them then, his chest filled to the bursting with the breath of eager battle. The rest of the men spread out, gladly conceding to Sturmund the honor of first blood.

When the shape burst through the treeline, Sturmund's

blade was already falling. He could not have stopped it even had he wished, such was the awesome power placed behind it.

Ghost lived up to his name, moving unlike anything human seemingly ever could, his lithe body bending under Sturmund's steel, the blade humming clean past.

Ghost's momentum carried him three steps more, where he collapsed into Culp's arms.

"Get hot water, bandages." Sturmund and Bitch shouted the commands as one, but Marney was already off to collect the necessary items.

Countless hours lost within the pages of books had not been wasted. Marney's knowledge of history and geography may have bored the men, but his familiarity with the body's inner structure had established him firmly as the sawbones of their group. Others certainly knew how to take apart the human frame; Marney alone could guess at how to put it back together. The men had given him experience aplenty putting theory into practice. From the look of the dark blood seeping beneath Ghost's hands, he gathered he would need every bit of it.

"Where is Hull?" Ghost's voice was weak, even for his gentle tones, and Sturmund had to lean close to hear.

"He's resting," Sturmund said. "He'll live."

Ghost gave a small nod, and grimacing suddenly, his body tensed in clear agony.

Sturmund struggled to pry pale hands from the bleeding gut so he could take stock of the wound. It was not as bad as he had suspected—any bloodshed seeming worse given the cadaverous pallor of this particular patient—but it was still bad.

The Captain carefully peeled off the hide Ghost had wrapped around his torso, and immediately a welling blackness seeped from the wound. Sturmund made efficient work removing the soiled rag and pressing a clean cloth to the savaged flesh—even so, the loss of blood was troubling.

"Marney," Sturmund shouted, not looking up. He was startled by the reply coming from so close.

"Keep pressure," Marney said, already returned from his medical stores. When he spoke, it was with the calm detachment of the practiced field surgeon, orders delivered precisely and in a tone that would brook no debate. Even Sturmund, now, was under the scholar's authority. "Bitch, you'll clean the knives as we go. Culp, hold him down at the shoulders. Captain, the legs. This is not going to be pleasant."

There would be no moving him. Where Ghost had fallen, he would lie, until he either got up again, or he did not. Patch saw to the tent, setting the stakes deftly, casting the tarp over the frame, bringing shelter to where it was most needed. Bitch managed the torches and the water.

They worked together, in relative silence, Marney doling out orders when required, but mostly the group proceeded in tacit understanding of what needed doing and when. It was not their first experience with the sight of blood.

"The forest—" Ghost said, rousing suddenly. He began to cough and hack, spittle and blood flecking his lips.

"Quiet, Ghost," Marney said. "Save your strength."

"You're going to need it," Patch offered coolly. He stood with his narrow shoulders hunched, arms crossed tightly in front of him as he watched events unfold.

Ghost resisted. He shook his head as far as his spasming muscles would allow, pain etched clearly on his face. He would be heard.

"In the forest . . . something terrible."

"We know," Sturmund said. And Ghost, looking up into

those firm eyes, seemed now relieved, his duty done. He had warned his companions; now they would see to the rest.

Bitch dabbed Ghost's forehead with a warm cloth when she wasn't busy sterilizing the crude instruments. Marney wielded the tools with uncommonly steady hands.

Having shared his report, Ghost had passed out almost at once, which was a blessing. They had run out of drink before the last battle, and a tough soul is not easy to quiet. Ghost, however, had excellent control over his own mind, and very willingly allowed himself to slip into the relative safety of the dark before the cutting and digging began. The mud-streaked walls of the tent were about to grow more soiled still.

Bleeding and infection—that was what was likely to do for any man injured in the field, and the signs were always clear, never subtle. A soldier would know soon enough if anything vital had been nicked inside his guts, the first minute a fair indicator of whether life would spill out with the rest of the gore.

Ghost had long since passed that threshold, and it stood to reason whatever was torn could be mended; whatever leaking, patched. Blood still oozed from the ragged flesh in dark, sticky trickles, but it was not the heart that pumped it now, merely the quivering muscles draining like a flank of meat hung upon a hook.

It would be hours, however, before any indication of infection might manifest. And while blood could be staunched, muscles sutured, flesh mended, nothing could abate the creeping death that came upon the soiled blade, the fetid tooth, the sullied earth. Where severed arteries break with brilliant jets and blooms of crimson spray, the angry wound brings slow fire to the poisoned veins. When a soldier sees the purple lips of festering flesh, he knows his time has passed.

Every culture has its own remedies for such sickness—poultices of slime-slicked moss and creeping lichen, spotted mushroom caps and night-flower blooms. The unscathed man knows the folly of such witch-doctoring—a hastened end or one more delirious still. But the stricken soldier, whose brow beads with ice-sweat even as his mind seethes, is not a discerning customer. Any offer of remedy, any promise of redemption, however mad or self-destructive, is one greedily seized.

Marney would have none of it, and in their camp the soldier either broke the blight with his own hard will, or rode the fever to the other side of the grave. Those gathered now looked on Ghost's shivering figure with doubt in their hearts. A moment later, Marney stuck his hand into the pale man's torso.

Half-way through scouring the wound, the scholar hesitated, his hands digging carefully into some pocket of flesh, the debriding of what seemed countless hungry splinters taking hours.

He felt blindly inside the wet and the warmth. No one scrutinized Marney's work. They'd seen more than their share of bloodletting in their time, and were content to let the old doctor work. But when the steady hands emerged, soaked to the wrists in deep red juices, all eyes were on him.

In his fingers was not the shred of bark, the splinter of burst wood. What he held was curved and sharp and jagged —and it came from no tree.

Marney handed the tooth to Bitch, who washed it in her store of boiled water. She clasped the fang between a pair of thin tongs and swished it through the basin, watching the blood and gore debride itself. When it had been washed clean of Ghost's innards, she held it up, and they all stared silently at it.

Patch appeared skeptical, Culp and Bitch merely uncomfortable. Sturmund, however—there was no one in that tent quite capable of explaining the covetous look Sturmund gave the tooth. Perhaps Marney could have offered some sage opinion, he knowing Sturmund longer than the others, but he had not bothered with the tooth. He was too busy with Ghost's guts to indulge a curious glance and chance the life of his patient.

By the time the last stitch was drawn through tired flesh, it was nearing dawn, still dark. Marney, who had worked tirelessly and with unrelenting focus, finally sat back, a weary sigh slipping through his cracked lips as he leaned against the stake of the tent.

"That'll have to do," he said simply, running a dark-stained hand over his brow and up through the sweat-dripped strands of his silvered hair.

No one asked if Ghost would live. He would, or he would not. There was no sense in speculating. Still, the satisfied smirk on the scholar's face told them they need not say their farewells just yet.

"Well cut me open and clean me out," Patch said, breaking the rare moment of calm. There was no ignoring the shit-eating way he spoke. He had found something worth bragging about—along with better spirits, it seemed.

The weary assemblage turned their collective attention to the smug face.

Patch squatted on the ground in his familiar vulture's fashion. Raised close to the one good eye was the mouth of a small leather satchel, his curved nose all but lost inside. They were all far too tired to speak, but Patch would not let them off so easily. He beamed, cheeks like apples, and waited to be asked.

Bitch sighed. "What, Patch?"

"Oh, nothing," he said, coyly as he could. "Just this."

He turned over the bag and the contents spilled out with a clatter of metal, the delicate tinkling of great value. Even in the low-light of guttering torches, the gold warmed the tent with its pooling luster. Yet despite the gleam it cast over the men's faces, their features grew only dark and hungry.

Sturmund alone appeared unmoved by the sight of treasure—at least of the sort before them. He had fallen thoughtful long hours ago, very thoughtful as he left the tent and the company of men to stare at the whispering forest, his mind contemplating a different prize altogether.

19

It is the sinister property of gold which causes it to gleam brightest in the darkest of places. The earth knew of this mystery long before any man had ever walked her back, and so she coveted the glimmering stone deep within her breast, where none save she could bask in its secret light.

For this, she was hated.

Since time immemorial, men have begrudged the earth her spoils, taking axe and pick to bleed her veins of such uncommon wealth, moving mountains for a glimpse at the color below, killing neighbors for a few flakes of ore, betraying themselves for handfuls of rock.

For that is the power of the light which blinds.

Set on a table for all to see, the soft, almost liquid warmth gently glows, a share for every man, a radiance divided. But cupped inside of greedy hands, a sight for one alone, and see how such strange lights do grow, almost too brilliant to gaze upon, yet impossible to ignore.

Brightest of all burns the gold kept most hidden, held within the secret heart, the dark heart, for treasure buried there does not simply shine but burns as fire does. A man must be careful he does not covet over-long, for selfish flames do not care what flesh they eat.

But gold is merely one such pyre upon which men have thrown themselves throughout their long and sordid history upon the earth. There are other fires that burn in the hearts of men—just as scorching, just as deadly.

20

Sturmund rolled the ring between his fingers, pausing occasionally to examine the seal.

It was only one of many precious trinkets Ghost had seen fit to recover, but the signet had caught Sturmund's eye and held for him a value not of women or drink or ease—such things found no home in so austere a mind. What Sturmund craved was purpose, a whisper from the watchful gods of death to guide him on his certain path.

And what he took from the ring was their answer.

He did not recognize the arms—a dragon perhaps, or a snake. He rubbed the emblem with his thumb, scraped away the dirt with his nail, but the impression was worn nearly flat by time and uncommon circumstance. He would consult Marney in the morning if he cared enough to ask, but Sturmund did not need to know from whose Great House the ring had slipped, only that it had fallen from lordly fingers. That was a fine thing to the grim warrior's mind. For if the beast could kill a nobleman, the beast could kill a hero.

And that interested Sturmund greatly.

Holding the band out to the candlelight, Sturmund watched the way the delicate metal absorbed the faint rays, seemed to radiate, to throb between his fingers.

If the gold called to him, Sturmund paid no heed, deaf as he was to its language, the whispered promises and idle temptations.

In his other hand, he held the fang. Next to the gilt metal, it seemed a grim trophy. Two rare specimens, each worth dying for in their own way—to the right man.

Where the ring grew warm between the calloused fingers, the tooth remained chill to the touch. Serrated on both sides, sharp as obsidian, crooked like a withered finger, the fang belonged to nothing Sturmund could put face to—though when he lay head to earth later that evening, his mind would try to unsettling result.

Much depended on the next few hours, and Sturmund hated himself for the doubt he had allowed to creep into his mind.

The men were tired and worn, true; but months of strife had also hardened their bones, tempered their nerves. These were men Sturmund had chosen, men he had fought with, men who had outlived all others. They were warriors, and Sturmund, better than most, knew where the journey was taking them.

With some regret, he thought back to the tensions earlier in the day—of Patch and Culp and Bitch—and to all the strain of the long days before. His men were restless, their souls wandering from that great and noble path first trod by their forebears, proud men who fought with honor and died with passion on their lips.

In the end, it was no hard choice at all: Sturmund was their Captain, his duty to lead. He had allowed his pack to stray—no more. Sturmund closed his fist around the tooth and, as the pale moon hugged the horizon, set himself to planning.

The gold ring dropped to the dirt of the tent, where it would remain, forgotten, for time out of mind.

21

A fox, copper-colored, sinewy, scurried along through familiar brush in unfamiliar times. Pointed ears rose slowly, very slowly, above dark foliage. Strange scents were on the wind that night, strange voices all around.

The forest lay in a state of unnatural fixedness. Hardly a creature stirred that was not seeking cover for the evening. The hunt, it seemed, would have to wait, an entire forest choosing slow hunger over quick death.

Somewhere in the woods roamed a beast.

Long generations of bird and wildcat had come and gone since the last awakening, no forest creature born of a time when the beast had walked the trees.

Still, they knew.

Some part of themselves, a hereditary past shared like folklore, had carried through, filling their hearts and minds with instinctive, essential fear.

And as the shadow of a dark world fell over the woods once more, life receded at its advance.

The little fox sank onto its paws, its soft belly barely flush with the wet ground as it listened to the growing thunder. Through the rain and the wind, the beast tore, a storm within a storm. The ground shook at its approach, but the fox remained—its heart, as its legs, urging flight.

The fox had known but two seasons since its birth—both of them hard. Nature had proved a cruel mistress, an indifferent replacement for the mother the wolves had taken. The copper fox bristled, wiry hair standing on end along a bony spine, sharp teeth bared toward the thrash of hooves.

A little copper fox sat in a rainy wood unwilling to yield the way. On came implacable Death, over trail and brush, through shadow and rain, blind hunger raving on its lips.

Fierce little claws dug into soft mud; fragile muscles tensed and braced. And over its world, the darkness swelled, high above the tiny creature, crashing downward with graceless violence.

The little copper fox closed its eyes.

The beast continued through the forest, thunder trailing heavy hooves, a path of broken trees and pummeled earth stretching forever in its wake. Along the way the beast had come lay a ruination of green; along the way the beast had gone lay a ruination of green.

Nothing stirred within the wreckage.

And when the thunder had faded and the earth had fallen still, only the rain disturbed the silent brush—until a little copper fox opened its eyes and raised a trembling head. Peering out from its thicket, around which all lay flattened, it began to breathe once more.

And on small and thankful feet, it ran.

22

There was little sleep that evening in the few hours that remained before the dawn. Bitch and Culp had shared the watch, their solemn shapes slim comfort to the rest of the careworn camp. Only Ghost slumbered truly, his whole being devoted to mending his wounds. The rest of the men found their evening thoughts more troubled than usual. In the morning, Ghost would share his report, but until then, fitful dreams and unearthly speculation presided over the silent encampment and its restless men.

Bitch had not once lifted her eyes from the looming forest since taking her sentry post. She had earned her rest, she and Patch both, but had insisted on standing guard. She knew sleep would not find her that night, so instead she listened to the patter of rain upon her cloak and thought dark thoughts.

Icy rain streamed down her dangerous face, over flared nostrils and tight-pressed lips. Inside the high leather boots water pooled, numbing her toes and setting her jaw on edge. The world around her had fallen to mud.

Beneath her hood, Bitch's eyes were slits, her glare for

the shadowed woods merciless. There was anger in her bones, hardened into the marrow of her being, aching always. The anger, it seemed, had always been there—just as the scars that marred her gut had seemed always to exist. Surely there was a time before the rage and the hate had swallowed her, before drunken savages had pinned her down and ripped from her womb the twitching purple form. But if there ever had been such a precious time as that, Bitch could scarcely recall.

Under cover of falling rain, wrapped in the folds of a sodden cloak and sheathed in the heavy fabric of shadow, Bitch, for the first time in ages, brought a hand to her stomach and wept.

She did not like to be reminded of what it was to be powerless at the hands of monsters. Whatever lurked in those woods had frightened her, and had not Patch been there to keep her to her duty, she knew she might have fled.

She hated Patch for her own weakness, as she hated the thing deep in the woods for its strength. In the morning she would put the shame behind her, but just then, in those lonely, brooding hours, she raged.

NEW LEAF

Three events have taken place in the span of as many days that warrant, I feel, at least a passing mention.

Hatch killed Foundling over a dispute with the horses. Hatch accused our hairless friend of seducing his stallion—much to my regret, I can confirm this, my tent abutting the stables; however, I took no part in either argument. Foundling denied the charge, but Hatch gave one look to the way the man hobbled out to breakfast and buried the axe in that shiny pate right then and there. Captain asked me to arbitrate. Hatch got the lash, and I set his stallion free, it having served its time, I felt.

Also, Sinner has run off, but there is nothing new there. We heard the howls last night, and found his tent empty this morning. He took nothing with him, not even the clothes on his back; we found those piled in the corner. If he tarries much longer, he'll have to catch up with us on his own.

Which brings me to the second strange tiding: we break camp tomorrow for the Marshland trails, of all places. Rider came this afternoon, from Overland, brought a contract from the mayor there about some bandits supposedly hiding in the swamps. I had to wonder if we were sought out special, or if the rider was just asking anybody who looked like they had a death wish.

We all know the rumors of the Marshlands—fish-people, mer-creatures, all manner of swampy abomination. Captain says Hull is to be kept a very close eye on, though he did not specify as to why. Regardless, it is going to be very dangerous going, and now we must likely do so without our best fighter in Sinner. Although I must confess, it is getting to the point where I am not sure if I feel safer in that wild-eye's company, or with him off on some crazed roving.

Strange Bob, as usual, has gone off in search of his brother. I told the Captain that one day they won't come back. They'll take to the woods like the madmen they are and eat whatever sorry passersby they happen upon. Who knows, perhaps one day we may even be contracted to put the poor souls out of their misery—though if history tells us anything, it's that the lunatics will outlive us all.

That brings me to the last, and somehow least welcome, piece of news of the past few days. It involves the woman—such as she is. She returned again, at the tavern. That marks the third time in as many weeks that she's shown up where we are. Captain seems indifferent to her, but I know he's starting to grow wary. Can't say I blame him. There is something very wrong about her.

—Personal Journal of Marney, Scholar

Addendum: Patch, I am aware you've been going through my pack, which means you'll no doubt be reading this. It may interest you to know that you're a great, big cunt, and the next time you need an ointment because you've rubbed your prick raw, I'll be sure to give you fire-jelly instead.

Still no sign of Sinner. We're only a week's journey from the Marshlands, and I can tell the Captain is doing his best to make the miles last. He, too, knows the value of our missing man. He won't wait forever.

Tonight we camp under the stars. Captain's orders. He says the men are getting soft bedding up at the inns. That is no doubt the truth, but I can't also help wondering if he is not also trying to avoid the she-devil. He can't stop her from joining the revel at the taverns we find, but only a fool would try to come upon our camp uninvited.

One of my texts has gone missing. An illustrated manual of mer-creature anatomy. I had wanted to brush up on local fauna before we hit the marshes. It's mostly speculation. Scarcely worth its parchment in coin or helpful information, but it's mine. I've never misplaced a gods-damned thing in my entire life, and when I catch the little shit that's pilfered from me...

Patch swears up and down he had nothing to do with it. My suspicions of him deepen by the day. I will put a few drops of slow-poison in his mash, see if we can't coax the truth out. A couple of days of bloody shits does wonders to distract the liar from his game.

Girl gives me the creeps. Showed up at the tavern, was just watching us as we drank. Seemed to catch Patch's eye. He doesn't like it when they tell him no, and this one's looks were shouting it across the barroom. I hope she doesn't let him get her alone, though for whose sake I worry, I'm not sure.

The rest of the night went off without much trouble. Hatch was in good spirits—drank till he passed out and shat himself, then woke up and started the process all over again. I think he misses Foundling. He came up to me later, pulling at his third pair of trousers—I didn't know where he was getting them until I caught one bare-assed fellow cowering in what I thought was the privy. Anyway, he said to me, "Marney, I shouldn't a done for Foundling like that. My horse was a slut, and we all knew it."

I made the mistake of agreeing; Hatch called me judgmental and stormed out of the barroom. At least he was out of my hair.

All the while that damn girl kept staring at us, as if she were taking stock. It's one thing to give an admiring glance, but the way she was glaring—it wouldn't do. By the end of the night, she had eyes only for the Captain.

But we'll put her out of mind, and move on down the road in the morning. If she turns up again, I don't know what might happen, but it won't be good for her.

I ink this entry with a bold hand, for I never wish to forget this date, not that I think I ever could.

She beat the piss out of him. I mean, the woman kicked that one-eyed jackal so hard in the gut that he actually pissed his trousers in the middle of the barroom. A woman! We have all sworn a vow never to let him live it down.

Sturmund sent her on her way. Patch was all red-eyed anger and oaths of vengeance, but I could see it in that beady little orb of his: he was damn glad she had gone by the time he had dried off. He was in no shape for a brawl, especially with something as feral as that creature.

She went, but her look told us all that she would return. I can't for the life of me figure what it is she wants from us. It's certainly not company. Thankfully, we are off for the Marshlands in the morning. Whatever her motives may be, I very much doubt she'll be following us into that squishy hell. I think that we've seen all we shall of that mean-faced vixen.

We proceed without Sinner and Strange Bob.

Two days in this filth. No sign of the bandits. Plenty of signs of life. We could build walls around our camp with all the fishy-flesh we've had to hack up, but I honestly think the bodies are attracting more attention from the bigger things we hear sloshing around out there.

We are overwhelmed by the sheer size of the marshes. I don't think any of us had expected anything so sprawling and dense. My maps aren't worth shit. The water here just lies in great gods-damned pools of green-slicked piss. There's no draw or movement to them, no tide or flow to give us any sense of direction. Just soggy, fly-riddled lagoons; greedy, sucking mud; and sodden vines on moldering trees.

What this company needs is a good gods-damned tracker. I keep telling the Captain as much, but even now he does not value any skill that places sneaking over flat-out aggression. One day, I hope he may see sense. Regardless, we all now know how carefully we must proceed. I am heartened to see how focused the men have remained, even young Patch.

There is hope for them yet.

Horse-fuckers and fish-fuckers. I've never known the like. Hull has apologized profusely—to me, to the Captain—but gods almighty, the smell. I think it will be with me to my dying day. Patch quite literally burst something from the laughter, and Hull broke the man's nose for all his sympathy. Patch can go sit on a thorn tree for all I care, but we've got to get Hull sorted, for our own sake, if not his. I am off now to find some night-blooms. I don't know if it'll help with what's itching Hull, but at least it should soften the odor.

And at a time when we need to be on our guard, this is what we have to deal with.

We found the bandits. What was left of them.

I didn't recognize it as human, but Patch pointed out the first of the severed cocks that day. Apparently, whatever ate them didn't care for the stringier parts. As we waded deeper, we found a dozen more, or rather they found us. The more we tried to swim away from them, the more eagerly it seemed they wished to brush up against us. It was a very discomforting experience. Patch threw one of the soggy things at Culp, and I had to save the boy from a drowning.

Hair, too. They didn't eat the hair. Great masses of it drifted on top of the water. You should have heard Hull scream when a particularly tangled mass of it got on him. I can't say I blamed him. What kind of creature eats tooth and bone, flesh and fat, but not cock and hair? We did not intend to find out.

We fished a couple of rings and one odd necklace from the muck that would stand as proof of our claim. We will press on the way we have been going, and send a rider the long way back for our fee for services rendered. All we have to do now is get the fuck out of here.

We're out, but Culp is all kinds of bruised up. We haven't stopped marching for hours. I think we all wanted to leave that place as far behind as we could for one day.

It was one of the most terrifying things I have ever seen, the way it just grabbed us all, each and every one of us, and pulled us down. Those hands, I can still feel them. They were so small. They were children's hands. I still don't understand if it was all one creature or many all rolling on top of one another.

All I know is that it was soft and mealy, and stood no chance against our steel. The men fought well. I know the Captain would say as much. Sharp minds and sharp blades made quick work of it. I must have had seven of those wriggling freaks on my spear. Not my record, but not bad for an old man all the same.

It was the big one that gave us the trouble. I did not think to check the trees. None of us did. And when it came crashing down behind us—the road, dry and safe, even then in sight—well, we could have all shat. I think Hatch actually did, though little surprise there.

I've seen plenty to churn my stomach in my years, but

the sight of that thing standing in the middle of that lake, just breathing and staring dumbly—that made my blood run cold. And when it started to roll towards us, fast as it did—well, that's going to stay with me for some time.

Leave it to Culp, though. I'm not sure it had a mouth, or even a face, but I think that putrid mass of swamp actually was surprised to see our man running its way. Gods, that was a good fight to see. Forget cocks and hair, there wasn't anything left of that monster when Culp got through mashing its guts.

But we're out, and Sturmund seems happy enough, even if he is sullen that Culp was quicker on his feet than he this time.

And another thing, that damn woman is still following us. I spotted her some leagues back, just making her way along our tracks. We can't seem to shake her. How *she* made it through the marshes unscathed, I don't know, except to say that we must have pretty much cleared the way. Culp says she's a banshee. He might not be so wrong. All I do know is I need a drink.

Oh, and guess where I found that missing text. Half the pages were stuck together when I got it back. I could kill that Red brute.

I have never seen the Captain so angry, and on a night we were meant to celebrate another contract lived through. She was lucky he did not cut her in half. At least now we know her mind. But to call Sturmund a coward—it was not the wisest play for one who wishes to join our company.

To her credit, she did not back down. Not when Patch told her to fuck off, not when Culp, face bruised like an old apple, showed her his back. Even Hull turned surly at the sight of her pleading eyes—for that is what they were, we now knew—though he was focused more on itching his balls than what was going on around him that night. Hatch was the only one to lay hands on the woman; I think he had just meant to show her the door. I'll have to ask him his intentions if he ever wakes up. She savaged him something fierce.

That's when the Captain put her down. Two hard strikes, that was all—nothing wasted, no lesson was meant, only a final message. I think she was surprised it was he who finally did for her; they had been making eyes at each other all evening. There wasn't a shred of romance in the looks, not from either of them, but there was no denying the intimacy. But he'd had enough; we all had. So down she went.

Something about a woman wanting to walk the path just didn't sit right with any of us. If she wanted to die, there were plenty more pleasant ways to go about it. If she wanted to kill—well, no one was stopping her; she just couldn't do it with us. Too wild by half. She'd have gotten us all killed—sooner rather than later, I have no doubt.

We left her on the floor where she fell, but the fight had gone out of us all. We quitted the tavern soon thereafter for more private drinking. She'd wake, eventually, but she'd wake alone. It was the last kindness we were prepared to offer her.

I am more ready for rest than I can ever remember having been. Seeing that thoughtless woman, it has disturbed me. Would any of us have chosen these same paths had we the means to unwind the clocks, to turn back all these years of hurt and blood? I am a fool to even write such words. Yet to see that desperate light in her eyes—she does not know what she asks. She should look for a man, bear children, carve out some manner of tranquility, if not happiness. For the first time in my life, I feel old.

I am turning out the light now.

Captain sought my counsel in the early hours, still dark. Woke me from a dead sleep. I can't recall the dream I was having, but the sweat on my brow told me I was better off waking.

He sat beside my bedroll, and even through the gloom, I could see the troubles in his eyes.

"Who am I to say?" That is what he asked me; that is how he began and ended the conversation.

It was no great mystery, even to my sleep-sodden mind. He was speaking of the woman, and of his handling of her. Not the strikes, for she deserved as much. It was the way he had pushed her away, the way we all had, that had eaten away at his rest that evening.

"You are the Captain," I told him. "If it is not for you to decide, then who?"

He just shook his head and rested his eyes a moment. I stared at him then, the man I knew, the proud youth I had known before that. They were the same person, and he was just as hard on himself now as he had ever been. I truly admire this man, and I can never be but grateful for the strange chance that brought us together. I might have been a general had we never met; now I know I shall be something greater still.

When his answer came, I was unsurprised, for my heart had whispered as much to me in those late hours. Still, I felt wiser for the hearing.

"It is greater than any of us, this path." He had spoken so

softly, so reverently in this hushed tent, while all around us dwelt in slumber, that I could not help but feel the stir of the sacred. The soft-footed gods had stopped in to listen, had sat beside us on the dirt of the tent and considered alongside me the man and his words, waiting, as I did, on his decision. "I may lead the men, but the path leads us all. Who am I to say?"

That was all he said.

I watched him go. I had not needed to share my mind with him, to tell him how strongly I agreed. He came not for assurance, but as a courtesy, perhaps.

He walked off into the evening, nothing but the thin tunic to keep the cold night air from his bones, and disappeared along the roads back. I knew who he was looking for, and I knew who he would find.

I will close my eyes once more, and wait to see what the morning brings us.

Today, we welcome a new member.

I do not deny that I have been wary of her, as I think we all have been. There is so much pain in her, and pain leads to recklessness. The desire to hurt or be hurt—the creature that suffers makes no distinction, as long as it will distract from whatever eats away at it.

But I am the surgeon of this camp, and I have seen every manner of cancer and toxin. What burns in her veins is direful stuff, indeed. Still, there is not a man among us who has not bled in my presence. I can confirm, at least to this silent parchment, that such burning stuff courses through us all.

We Burn Our Dead

The men have accepted her, or they will, in time. Patch had a right good laugh when she told us all her name.

"You certainly are," I believe his words were.

And lo and behold, our Sinner is back, still naked as the day he was hatched. Imagine my surprise. Bob came, too, whistling strange tunes and telling peculiar tales. I told them if they were expecting a share of the purse from our latest adventure, they could choose between twelve severed cocks and a mountain of hair. Captain said otherwise, and told me to make certain the two were paid an equal share.

"The warrior honors those who have helped him along the path," he told me later, over a drink. "How many times have Sinner and Strange Bob saved our lives? How many times have you or I saved theirs? We are all of us linked, and so we all of us share—in the glory and the pain; we should relish the taste of both."

He surprises me sometimes, our Captain. I could write for days about the man. I've known him long enough; his father, too. It certainly would make for an interesting tale. I wonder if any of my camp-mates would believe it.

But alas, it seems I have run out of parchment. This has been an eventful season. I must go and strip some bark.

23

Culp's watch proved uneventful. Bitch had woken him with a kick to the ribs, harder than had been needed, but Culp had glimpsed the fury in her eyes and so had let the roughness pass.

The monotony of the rain-soaked night was broken only once in those quiet hours. Hull cried out in his sleep, a haunted, child-like wail that all pretended not to hear. A moment later he was silent and would remain so until the dawn.

Culp despaired of the wasted hours. He bore the rain and the cold as would any warrior worth his salt—with defiance to the elements, with relish for the pain. With his blade-shorn scalp and fist-ravaged nose, Culp seemed a warrior born for the field. Of all the men to have served under their Captain, Culp was the fighter closest to Sturmund's cut. Brave, rugged, solitary—two men carved of stone, giants on the field of battle, mere shadows in the peaceful hours. But there ended the resemblance.

For all his quiet strength, Sturmund possessed a mind always moving, always searching, where Culp's so often remained at rest, no deeper hunger than physical contest driving him onward. So when Culp gazed into the treeline and saw the shadows and the darkness and nothing more, he did not wonder what lived within the gloom. He had not been in those woods, and held no strong convictions about the matter. He had not liked it when the unseen thing had screamed and threatened, but he had never any love for things that hid and crept. If it would not bring itself into the lists, it was no thing at all.

Culp considered the forest a moment longer, spat rain from his mouth, and turned his mind to thoughts of breakfast.

24

Sturmund had given no indication life should continue on any differently than before. If the morning came and their Captain willed it, they would pack up their gear and their wounded and carry on, down other roads, towards other fights.

They had each lived too long a life to have dwelt overlong on revenge, and knew the only gold that had value was gold that could be spent. Hull and Ghost looked both to survive—no debt needed collecting on that score. And whatever had bested two of their own was likely something that could have bested three, and none was eager to test the theory. There were easier ways to earn a living, and each nursed the secret hope that the morning sun would help their Captain see as much—none of them truly believing he would, or even could.

Sturmund's men did not all think of themselves in the same proud way as their Captain saw them. When Sturmund studied his men, the weight of his eyes upon them were as his own convictions—heavy and unyielding—and the thoughts that shone there always the same. He wanted for them all a warrior's life, and somewhere within that, a warrior's death. Nothing else would do.

Yet not all who fight are fit to claim such honors. A sword can just as easily be wielded by a brigand as a hero, and often more easily, for the brigand is not hindered by the awkward heft of principle as he grapples. But Sturmund, with his hardened, searching eyes, must have seen something promising in the faces, in the hearts, of the desperate men who came to him, else he would never have taken them into his fold and unto his protection. Through the Captain's example, they each, in their way, tried to live up to his lofty expectations. They did not always succeed.

They were soldiers, mercenaries, blades for hire. They were fighters and killers and men of war. They were feared by all who had ever crossed steel with them, but they were not Sturmund's warriors—not *truly* warriors—not yet, at least.

But the day was fast approaching.

25

In a distant and forgotten part of the forest, the rushing beast clambered to a stop, clouds of soil swirling in its wake, trails once green trampled into unrecognizable, irreparable mire. With deliberate effort, it raised its gruesome head, cords of muscle thick as rope bulging as they stretched. Crust-covered slits quivered as the pale beast drew breath into its dripping nostrils. On hungry, smacking lips, it savored the breath of the wind. All the secrets of the forest laid themselves once more bare to the ancient master.

When the creature returned to the gloom of its burrow, it found the piece of meat gone. It stomped into the empty cave, lowering its lofty head beneath the rough shelf of rock above. Bone crunched and snapped as it trod into the chamber, gold and silver trinkets bent under its passing weight. It stood before the spot of earth where the tender flesh had been left to soften and heaved a heavy sigh into the empty hollow. A brooding, wounded lament filled the cavern.

With a sickening roar the beast shook its pale hide, dislodging scraps of angry steel from an earlier insult. The weapons clattered to the pile below, more rubbish for the heap. The wounds did not trouble the beast. They would heal in time—in time. What pained it truly was the absence of blood to drink, of flesh to chew. A menacing growl belched from its seething bowels as blind fire burned within its skull.

The flesh had escaped. There had been a great quantity of flesh that night. Long years had passed since the beast had come upon such plentiful flesh. It would have made a worthy meal.

The thoughts were poison to its mind, turning evil dreams worse, breeding madness and malice, for beyond the edge of the forest the beast knew it could never tread. For all its power and all its fury, to walk through open fields was a thing denied it—by gods or nature, it had never known. And so, the flesh had escaped, for the beast knew, through long experience, no mortal man ever returned who once made it out of that wooded hell.

For a very long time, the beast remained still, deep in the shadows of the cavern, monstrous face turned to blank stone walls. Time held no mastery over a creature that could wait forever to take its next breath. There was no defeat for one which could bide eternal, until the flesh withered and sloughed from an enemy's bones, until the face of the earth weathered and washed clean of all that had offended. Everything fell to time while time, surrendered only to the beast. And within its mindful wrath, it would wrap itself in the solace of knowing that the flesh of men always rots.

26

In the morning, the rain had stopped, and Hull had died. The sun was bright and cold, the field soggy and brown.

Patch went out early and slew a cottontail. He did not go near the woods, but doubled back along the group's upward course and on the rocky slopes found the lean critter and felled him from an impressive remove. When he returned, he handed the limp-necked rabbit to Bitch, who did not at first understand.

The gold had cheered him some, but Patch had not yet regained his full easy deportment. He answered Bitch's questioning glance with a sullen nod towards the sallow-faced corpse Marney and Culp had dragged away from the fire. Then she understood.

She used her own blade, slit the rabbit's throat, and let the black blood spill into a basin. Culp and Marney watched her bring the bowl to the motionless figure, Marney elbowing Culp when he realized, both men turning awkwardly away.

She bathed the hair carefully, delicately, drawing the straw-colored strands through her red-stained fingers, watching as fresh life was breathed back into the proud locks. Sturmund watched from the mouth of his tent. When she finished, he went out to join her.

"He died in his sleep." Sturmund sounded mournful, and Bitch knew he regretted the manner of the death, not the loss itself.

"He fought bravely," she said, not looking up. "You should have seen him, Sturmund. He was everything you would have wished him to be." She thought of the hammer and the mighty cry, the willing desire of an old warrior to face death and feed it his steel.

"Almost," Sturmund said.

"We dragged him off the field," she said, a hint of testiness in the voice. "He went kicking and yelling. He wanted nothing more than to die in that . . . thing's embrace."

Sturmund nodded, his eyes hard on her, as always. She rose and stood before him, meeting the gaze undeterred.

"What will you have us do?" She spoke with a soldier's dispassion. Had Sturmund pointed over the cliff, she would have marched.

Bitch watched as her Captain's cold, blue eyes passed from her down to Hull's still body then finally over to the treeline. The woods were quiet that morning, looking as woods so often do—placid and aloof. One could almost have been forgiven for not thinking there to be a monster somewhere inside its sprawling labyrinth.

"We commit our dead to the sea," Sturmund said. "And then we find his killer."

"We *burn* our dead," Bitch said.

Sturmund pulled his eyes from the woods with some difficulty. He was not prepared for what faced him.

"We burn our dead," she repeated.

Sturmund shook his head. "He did not fall in battle."

Bitch made to speak. Sturmund's raised hand silenced her.

"Hull was born of the sea. On her back, he slew his first man. He spoke of this often to me, when we both sailed her waters." And in Sturmund's eyes Bitch thought she could see the memory rippling, the strife and crash of an ocean battlefield, the true birth of the old warrior she once knew.

She nodded, and later that day, they rolled the bundled figure off into the blue where it struck, heaved, and, finally, sank. The watery grave of an old salt. The first of them to die that day.

SEA SALT

For one mad moment the ship listed so severely that the young man could have reached from where he braced at the deck-wall and touched a raw and blistered hand to the black waters that even then struggled to bring them down. Staring at their destruction, he could not help but think it beautiful, though he would be alone in the sentiment.

"Man the line, you lazy cur."

The ugly voice cut through the gale; the eager crop tore a similar path through the young man's flesh.

Only the smack of boiled leather against skin returned to the officer's ears, for not a sound emerged from the young man's lips, either at the bite of the lash or the sting of the insult. Scowling at the deck hand's back, the officer raised his arm for another demonstration, hoping this time for the courtesy of a cry.

"I said heave, you whore-son." And the lash came down.

Even after long and crowded years, the stamp of angry foot on the salt-slicked deck would be a memory fresh and favorable to the young man's mind. Neither the snapping sail or the howling wind could conceal the coming storm, and the officer half-turned to greet it, fire flashing in his spiteful eyes, lash-hand stalled in disbelief.

No love had been lost between the officer and the men of his charge, the course of their months-long voyage charting ever-deeper into savage waters. But that was nothing new upon the ocean waves. Restless seas and restless men—it was a story as old as salt itself.

Nor was the zealous discipline that righted the listing man a feature worthy of comment beyond the grumble into an evening grog. Blood paid as much a part of a sailor's passage as the sweat of his tired brow.

But when the wrathful lieutenant had ventured to defame the honor of a mother, he trespassed too far upon the strained graces of his tired men. The hand that rose to the young man's defense did so with more than entirely selfless intent.

Even as the deck hand moved in his own defense, the fellow shipman's fist reached out from within the stormy air and blew like the crush of wave against the sharp cheek, blood misting in the salty spray.

The officer dropped to the deck, his assailant quite pleased with himself.

The satisfaction proved short-lived.

The red brute looked down and spied what he could of the blade, three inches jutting from the lieutenant's heaving chest, at least twice as much buried within. The officer's wild eyes darted between the two sailors, the desperate look within the fading gaze an unpleasant tonic of terror and rage.

"You don't fool around, do you, young master?" said the helping hand.

"A man who raises his fists must always be prepared to face his end. A man who raises his tongue gets no such advantage."

The red-haired sailor gawked at the young man, not even the raging squall able to overshadow the earnest passion flaring in the cold blue eyes.

"And that's all well and good, but if you don't help me roll this sack of shit overboard, we'll be joining him soon enough."

It was easy work. The officer hadn't had much fight in him before taking a blade to the lung; as things stood, he could do little more than gurgle and moan as the two shoved his trembling body over the deck-wall.

"Man overboard," the red sailor cried.

The two stood panting, more from the effort to keep their footing upon the rolling deck, than from grappling with so unequal a foe. The red-beard took the moment to size up his fellow sailor.

The lad was new, to their vessel and to the sea, if he was any judge. The young sailor had come aboard at the last port, which struck the red-beard as odd; those vibrant eyes and rich blond hair could mark him only as a Northerner, yet they were a thousand miles from those cold reaches. How the lad had found his way so far from home was anybody's guess. He made a note to question him later; then, recalling the fast feet and the faster blade, he reconsidered. In the end, he was just glad at having made a friend after so long a voyage without one.

For the youth's part, he merely saw in the red-beard a willing fist and an eager fire, with brawn enough to back up both.

"They call me Hull," the red beard said, with a pat of his broad chest.

"I am Sturmund," the young man answered, their hands clasping one another's forearms, forging the first link in a chain that would stretch across the kingdom and to the other side of hell.

"Sturmund?" Hull said, taken aback. "You mean someone actually named you after—"

"Get back on the lines, you shit marks," cried a disheveled officer, as he scrambled down from the bridge. And just like that, order was restored from the midst of chaos.

It was only the loss of a deck hand or linesman, or any other of the hundred enlisted men aboard, that would be felt when the seas needed taming. The loss of an officer was a problem scarcely noticed, and repaired as easily as slapping a hat upon the nearest rascal's head. Only ignorance of this knowledge kept the masses from taking the ship, as it kept the entire kingdom's farmers from storming the gates of the great Keep itself.

"Aye, sir," Hull called back. "Right you are." And together the newly-formed pair took hold of the lines and fought their way through the storm.

"Fucked a fish, they say."

"A fish?" Sturmund was working in the larder, helping the cook to salt the surplus of the day's catch. The maelstrom had passed, and the riled waters left in its wake offered consolation to the shaken sailors in the form of abundant seas.

He was surprised to hear so fine a fighter spoken of so poorly. It was only later he would come to understand that Hull, despite his years at sea, was still but a junior mate among the crew, subject to the whims of any scoundrel with enough stripes on his sleeve. For all his heart and all his passion, Hull would always be, it seemed, lowest man—and all because a few officers had taken a dislike to the mighty sailor's hair.

"Well, not a long-tail or a shark or anything like that. That would be ridiculous. This was one of them—what do you call 'em—an octopus. That's why we call him Fish-Fucker."

"I thought he was known as Hull."

The scrawny cook cackled. "Hull? He tell you that?"

Sturmund did not answer. He did not care for the cook's manner. Where Hull chose to stick himself was of no concern to the young sailor, except when it came to how readily the man had thrust himself into the recent skirmish. The red-beard had acquitted himself well, and to Sturmund, had risen as high as any man who stands his ground—and, consequently, a great deal higher than any other aboard the vessel.

"Hull," the cook repeated. "That's a good one. But not for our Fish-Fucker." Here the cook's idle slurs turned merely savage. "Damn Reds, bunch of inbred good-for-nothings. Probably reminded him of his sister, that octopus did."

And with that stinging vitriol, the cook picked up his mallet and began mashing the pile of fish heads for chum. The relish with which he set himself to the task left no doubt as to where his thoughts lay.

The kingdom had no shortage of foul and unkind climes. Northerners kept the icy airs and frozen ground, accepting their lot with stoic indifference, their thick skins and hard hearts keeping out cold as well as comfort.

In the South, the marshes stretched like a patchwork

plague around the few mounds of dirt where so-called civilization had sprung up from the muck.

The storm-slapped Coast and jagged shores were left to the fishers and the gypsies, and the less said about that savage East the better.

All clung to their meager lot and spat in the face of any who claimed to have it worse. Still, if anything existed under the burning sun or spiteful stars to join together these disparate creatures in common thanks, it was that none of them had been born an Islander.

Desolate. Detestable. Deranged. When one spoke of the Islands, one spoke also of the Reds. There was no love on the whole of the mainland for one kissed by the mischievous fire. Ill-tempered and taking always too easily to offense, the ruddy clans of the far-flung rocks kept to their lonely shores and humble earthen burrows, to brood on their ill-fate and to curse the world, their neighbors, and themselves in equal measure. It was a rare day indeed when one of their number dared to test the loveless waters of the worlds beyond his shores; thick-hide, foolish head, and likely both, would be needed for the venture.

Sturmund had never before set eyes on an Islander until that evening before. He was glad of the meeting then, and thankful now for the lesson he had not at first realized he had taken from it.

"You misjudge him." Sturmund's words emerged from the heavy silence that each man had withdrawn to—the cook's, one of stewing contempt; the young deck hand's, a meditation on unexpected turns of fate.

Sturmund had not set off on his journey—alone and penniless, leaving behind friend and family both, forsaking inheritance in the hope of gaining one greater still—only to involve himself idly in the affairs of others. He intended to make something of himself through the journey, by the toil of his own hands to raise himself to greater heights than any who had come before him.

He was unsurprised then to find the voice of the warrior —the stony spirit he had long ago discovered nesting in his heart, this grim and faithful warden who had guided his actions and his course with clear and cutthroat command— urging him now to strange and unlikely action.

Sturmund did not argue with the spirit, confident it knew how best to keep him to the path; he merely raised his fist as his nature required.

"You—you—" The cook sputtered, hand clutching at his now-crooked nose, marveling off and on at the slick of blood that came away from it. "You'll get the lash for this, you will." He started to giggle from his nerves, unsteady as he looked about him and blanching when he realized how truly alone he was.

"I have already learned my lesson," the youth said indifferently. "But since we are here, you and I, let us make sure you have learned yours."

That night, a storm more fearsome than the last burst upon the lonely vessel.

Calm seas must follow riled wave.

Sailors cling to many gods and hold with superstitions numberless, with chains and baubles, totems and talisman enough to shame the mightiest savage-king. But all who sail the fathomless seas, from lowliest swab to grandest Admiral, find common footing upon this one simple truth: on the other side of every storm wall, though fire-lit and phantom-filled, lies a sea brighter than any which lay behind.

On the morning Sturmund was to receive his lashes, a brilliant vista unfolded before the aged vessel as she plowed through sparkling waters, under skies as rich and blue as antique sapphire. Forgotten almost entirely was the mindless maelstrom that had threatened their lives, menaced their souls the night before. White sunlight bathed the salt-stained timbers, adding luster where only dullness dwelt, grace where festered decay. The ship regained by day that pride which went again with every weeping night, and like the formless spray thrown by her heaving hull, rising as brilliantly as it fell, a stately air wrapped her old bones just long enough to fool the eye into believing.

"I will not suffer any man to bind me." The words sounded clearly upon the bright morning air, like a trumpet-call before the battle, a pronouncement and a challenge.

A grumble passed through the gathered crew. A lashing was a communal spectacle, a worthy distraction from the daily toil, when for a few brief moments, work-worn sailors could gather as one in looking upon the rare sight of him whose lot was worse than his own.

Sturmund's manner was not at all in keeping with the grand traditions of public shamings, and his notable lack of supplication left a bad taste in the rotting mouths of those assembled.

Sturmund stood by the mast, his back to the pillar where countless men before him had suffered similar chastisement. The wood was enriched with a patina of deep color, and before morning had passed to night, would be made more profound still.

"By gods, you will be bound," cried the officer supervising the whipping. He was a surly-mouthed creature with pockmarked features. Color seethed under his soiled collar at the defiance. "Take hold of him."

Sentiment was not on the youth's side, and the volunteers to the officer's call were many and willing. The first two hands to break from the crowd were not shy with their contempt. For his part, Sturmund was not shy with his own.

The Red watched from the furthest reaches of the assemblage. Wishing to offer the lad a familiar face during his ordeal, he had taken a position much nearer the mast, but as the crew continued to gather, he found himself driven further back with every callous shove and spiteful elbow. As it was, he could barely see the lad above the angry heads craning and bobbing throughout the crowd.

"I cannot see," Hull said, wishing to flatten the nearest ten men to better his view, but knowing the inevitable cost of such rebellion. He merely accepted his lot and continued griping. "What's happening to him?"

In the confusion, Hull managed to earn an answer from those not realizing who it was that had spoken.

"He's taken down the both of them," one swab called. "That uppity little shite."

"What?" Hull asked, disbelief cracking under a quick snort.

"And another one," called a linesman from somewhere above in the rigging.

"Can't of done," said Hull, first disbelief, then worry, coloring the heavy tones. If the lad had defied another order, and then had assaulted, what, half a dozen more shipmen? Well it did not bode well for the young sailor's prospects. Not one bit. "Crazy young buck."

A well of strange emotion sprang up in the Red brute's heart, such that at first he patted his chest vigorously, thinking the second helping of salted eel he'd snuck for breakfast had slipped his digestion, and only then realizing with even greater discomfort that he was afraid for the boy.

Though he still had no knowledge of the honor Sturmund had done him in crushing half the cook's features, Hull was already enough impressed by the lad's fighting spirit and frank demeanor to wish him better than a death by mob-beating. After all, he was the first in—how long?—to look at the Red without a hint of disgust in his eye.

Suddenly, it did not seem to Hull so important that he mind his place, that he duck his head when others turned his way. Just then, he only thought about helping the lad, and about how much he wished for a friend. Before he realized what he was doing, his iron grip had taken the nearest man by the shoulder and flung him clear over the gunwale. In the jeering confusion, none seemed to have noticed. Encouraged, Hull chanced again the technique.

"Red bastard," came and went the cry, as it swiftly descended into the rushing deep.

But his throw this time had not gone unobserved, and Hull was disturbed to find the eyes of a sailor some ways down the line staring straight at him. Hull scowled, an instinctive response to the terror that surged through him like lightening. He had been caught out. The sailor, however, did not cry to alarm, did not divert the crowd to the purpose of stringing up yet another man; he held Hull's attention, his dark eyes never leaving the Red's, then very softly, yet very clearly, the stranger nodded.

It was all the encouragement the Red needed, and he set off to help the lad.

Hull's cheeks took on the glow of childish delight as he leaned his burly frame into the swelling crowd. Slowly but implacably, a way was made by force. It felt wonderful to be doing something one loved. He plowed his way into the clearing he had dug for himself, stony fists ready to strike down the next man to stand in his way, the next bloody fool

We Burn Our Dead

to dare to challenge his right of passage. His blood was Red, was it not? And at that moment, it ran almost too hot for his thick veins to hold.

The loss of one or two of the crowd would have scarcely been noticed among the confusion of sailors storming the deck. Come evening, when roll was called, the missing men would be felt, but by then, who was to say how they had come to tarry. Perhaps they had gone grog-blind and made the wrong turn off one of the masts, or chanced to catch a note of some mer-wench's siren song and followed it the way to soggy death. Stranger things were known to happen on the shoreless seas, or so the sailors were wont to say.

No, a missing man or two, that could always be explained. A Red, however, never thinks further than his arm can cast, and given another moment's leave, Hull might have cleared half the deck. And by then, there would be little doubt as to which poor bastard would need stringing up. Luckily for Hull, it would not come to that, for the sudden cheers of the crowd stalled his progress and snuffed out the last of his flickering hopes.

The cheer came up, and Hull knew the lad had gone down. The burly brute craned his neck, and found from his new position, he could make out at last the stage on which the scuffle had taken place.

There were two piles of bodies, each several men deep from the looks of it. Only one of the piles was moving, elbows falling, fists striking madly. Reds were not prized for their wits, but even Hull could guess under which heap the boy now lay.

With a weary sigh, he accepted the loss and surrendered the hard-fought ground, letting the remaining crowd once more surge around him, shoving him back to the rear, where he leaned his heavy frame against the gunwale and stared out to the horizon, spying, as he did, two faint bobbing forms flailing in the distant waters, receding soon out of sight entirely.

"Get him up." The cry had fallen from frothing lips. The officer was dancing around the heap of fighters, arms waving and gesturing like a shaman working a wicked curse. "Stand him up and tie him down."

With much reluctance, the fighters gave up their man. To their surprise, the young sailor, though bloodied and more than a little battered, remained, it seemed, unbowed.

Sturmund pushed away the grasping hands, continuing to strike out, albeit with less vigor than before, any man who aimed to control him. The sight did much to silence the remaining jeers lobbed from the crowd, and even more to turn the sentiment, so strongly against the young sailor only moments before, into something almost akin to hope.

"Give him space," one hand said, waving still another back. And surprisingly, the crowd obeyed.

They watched silently, officer included, though that man's tongue was perhaps only tired from all the fire it had spat. The young sailor rose, unsteadily.

It took a long few moments for him to work up enough spit to get the words out, during which time a few lonely gulls called out from the empty skies above and the waves sloshed gently against the prow.

"I have broken your rules," Sturmund said, his voice hoarse but sure. "For that, I will be punished."

The officer slipped a scoff at the arrogance of the youth, but still had not found the words to voice his precise feelings on the matter. He stared along with all the rest.

"But you will not bind me," he continued, with a grave finality that none—men twice, thrice his years—doubted. They might beat him, might kill him or toss him overboard, but not a one among them had any lingering illusions about binding the young sailor.

At last, the officer found the words he had been looking for. "You cunting piece of gull-scum." Then, to the men gathered, "Cut him to chum."

Orders were orders. The blades drew, begrudgingly but no less slowly. Sturmund readied to meet his fate, fists raised, spirits with them.

"Belay that order." The call came not a moment too soon. The Captain's face was an unfamiliar sight upon the early morning deck, his roar was not.

Two dozen sailors lowered rusting cutlasses, chipped poniards, ugly cudgels, and one surly old mariner lay down his mop. An equal number of eyes, some beady, all bleary, turned to the upper balustrade.

"Proud lad," the Captain said, eyeing the bloodied youth below. "Foolish lad."

The Captain leaned over the rail, the rotting wood straining under the weight of his frame, a corrupted mass of muscle and mad will, the result of hard years running ships for ruthless men, until the day arrived when he had stolen enough of their gold to outfit his own vessel for voyage. In short order, he had poached the best men for his crew, and cut the throat of every former comrade who refused to join his cause. Here was a man who knew something about grit.

"The boy won't be bound. I can respect that." An ugly smile split the lips; uglier teeth revealed the true sentiment. "How many lashes?" the Captain asked of his staff.

The officer cleared his throat. "Twenty, Captain, but I would—"

"Double it." The voice was perfectly at ease. "And if he so much as bends his knee, if he for one moment tries to brace himself, you will cut off his cock and take out his eyes, and then every man aboard this ship will take a turn in whatever hole is free."

With that, the Captain turned and loped back into the humid darkness of his quarters.

"Aye, sir," the officer called, over the grumble from the crowd. A man might bear ten lashes and limp away; might survive twenty and be carried—but forty? The crew had already given up the young sailor for dead, some even then slipping away to lay claim to whatever effects they might find stashed in his berth.

"Now, boy," the officer said, turning round and drawing the lash's tails of boiled leather through his hands, "you will stand clear of the post. For if you lay one finger upon it..." He did not finish the thought, merely ran a slug-like tongue over his lips.

A sudden movement from the crowd surprised the officer, whose arm was even then ready to bring down the lash. Hull, too, was caught out, not simply because the figure had beaten him to action, but that he seemed to have a plan in mind. That was one step further than Hull had managed.

The man strode confidently toward the shirtless youth, who made no move to stop him. No one, in fact, made any move to stop the interloper, for he stalked with a purpose that parted the crowd as readily as had Hull's barreling heft, and with a bearing that held their sword arms at bay. Hull recognized him at once as the dark-eyed sailor who had earlier encouraged his aggression.

"Take a hold, boy," the man said as he reached the unfettered prisoner, offering up to him the piece of folded-up hide. "Bite down hard. It wont ease what's coming, but it'll spare your tongue the taste of its own meat."

Sturmund made no sign he would accept, but neither did the stranger give any indication that he would relent.

"There's no shame in being wise, son." The man spoke firmly, and the voice carried a resolve that pierced like a spear thrust. Sturmund, though glimpsing the hide warily, could not deny the good sense in the words.

He accepted the bit, and the stranger, satisfied in his efforts, slipped back into the crowd, and troubled Sturmund no more that day or all the rest of the voyage.

An instant later the lash came down.

"You're a king, aren't you boy?" Hull eyed the sturdy youth with some consideration. "I've found you out at last."

They had sailed in each other's company for the better part of three months, growing well-familiar along the way. Theirs was comfortable partnership, if not yet true friendship, though that did nothing to stop bonds much more profound from taking root. Witnessing the noble bearing with which the lad had taken the vicious lashing, not once stumbling or even bending his knee, had left one party decidedly more in awe of the other; and on discovering the reason that drove the lash, the proud Red had clasped a rough hand round his companion's forearm and swore an oath neither doubted would stand the test of years.

"Or a princeling, perhaps." Hull had needled the youth every day about his background, and got little and less for his efforts. The young man offered only what he wished, and not one word more.

"No, not a prince," Sturmund said. "Not any more."

Hull paused in his work, pink guts dangling from the opened fish-belly. He leaned closer.

"I gave all that up," the youth continued, not so much as

a hint of jest in the voice, "so I could swab decks and gut fish with you for the rest of my days."

Hull bellowed. "Mighty fine living, mighty fine."

Sturmund smiled, only faintly, and never showed his teeth in good humor. Still, Hull would remain the only living creature who could bring good humor to the dour man's heart.

"Well," Hull said after a breath, "there's something noble in you, lad. I'll bet my beard there were royals in your line somewhere up the way. You might think to have look one day. Who knows, you might be some bastard heir to all the land." Hull boomed again. "Although, a name like yours, perhaps it's wiser not to poke around too much."

The stern and sober look drew suddenly over the young man's face, catching his companion off guard, as it always did.

"The man who possesses himself," the young man said, his earnestness lending him an authority far beyond that which his years deserved, "is richer than any king."

Hull nodded, lopping off another fish head into a bucket. He seldom understood the lad, but he was glad to be worthy of the confidence. Now and again, he tried to repay the kindness with a tale of his own history.

"Have I ever told you the tale of how I slew my first man?"

"Many, many times."

"Well, would you like to hear again it or not?" the big man asked, suddenly snippy.

"A tale so bold," Sturmund said, "I shall never tire of hearing."

"A bright young lad you are. Stick with me, and we'll get along famously." A fishy slap on the back followed. "Now, if you're lucky and the mood suits, I may even tell you the tale of how I bedded the most beautiful lass on all the seven seas, and never you mind what the others say, she was *not* a mermaid."

"Rest assured, they do not say that."

"Eh, right. Good. Now then," the mighty Red said, setting the scene with a wide raise of his massive hands, "it all started, if you can believe it, with an octopus..."

27

Six remained, and so six set out. Yesterday, they had been seven, and before that a number greater still. But that day, they were six, and with proud Sturmund at their head, their number seemed legion.

In their past were taken kingdoms and kneeling chieftains, spoils immeasurable and glory profound. That they came that day in worn leathers and scuffed plate took nothing from them. A man does not need a crown to know himself a king, nor does the mighty warrior require any more than the steel in his hand and the steel in his heart.

They had each slipped into the forest from a slightly different approach, fanning out, a broad line moving as one. Sturmund would not have them underfoot of one another— in the tangled woods there was difficulty enough in getting out of one's own way. And so each man stepped of his own accord into the brush and the unknown, following no one, his first true step on the warrior's path now made alone.

They moved slowly, their footsteps muffled by strips of hide tied around their heavy boots. Marney had seen to it, at Ghost's insistence. It dulled some measure of sound, twigs crunching instead of cracking, dirt whispering underfoot instead of scuffing, but they none of them knew the art as well as Ghost, who even then, pained with every movement, every breath, never made a sound he did not wish heard. He had joined them without argument from the rest, simply dressing himself and his wounds, and appearing by the group as they readied for battle, falling in amongst them as if he had never been apart.

If a man can breathe, a man must fight.

These were Sturmund's words, and, as each new recruit came to the formidable Captain, they become his own as well—an inherited philosophy, an adopted path, a road not easily walked.

And if a man should fight, a man must win.

Before the man could become the warrior, before the compact was forged with blood and steel, Sturmund first recited the words, ensuring they were understood, his grave tones carrying more warning than welcome, for Sturmund understood what lay at the end of the long road, what with every lonely step the warrior courted.

Even when victory comes with death.

And some walked away, knowing the cost was more than their souls could afford. Better such men go. Sturmund said nothing and watched as they went, down different roads, to live different lives—where families and homes waited, but no glory ever dwelt.

For there is no living without death.

The words, like the compact, were inviolable, Sturmund's blade the certain justice of the oath-breaker. There was more to this warrior's code, but that was a lesson learned only in time, the unassuming motto more than enough for the fledgling hero's first steps along the blood-soaked path.

And there is no glory without blood.

Each of the six still surviving, those last of a countless and storied line, had entertained that day what they had come to know of the warrior's way—Sturmund not least of all. His watchful eyes had taken stock of the group as they prepared, oiling leather and testing straps, cleaning blades and donning plate. They had been silent, his warriors, but it had been a silence of calm and acceptance, no traitorous fear lurking amongst his flock as they readied themselves for war. And though none had seen it—and perhaps blessedly so—a triumphant glint had shone in the cold waters of Sturmund's eyes, because Sturmund knew a day was finally at hand.

As long as a man can breathe...

28

At first, the great beast would not believe.

It raised a dripping snout to the air and scoured, sucking deeply, powerful chest heaving and falling, as it hunted for the source. With a wet snort, it blew out the filthy stench, a puddle of viscous snot seeping down to bared teeth as it purged, again and again, what wafted on the distant wind.

Then it listened, the shell-like organs nestled safely within the sunken pits of its head throbbing with every whisper, every hum, however faint. It closed its sightless eyes, listening into places beyond the reach of other ears— the whispered wings of the delicate insect, the solitary creak of an aged tree, the lone sigh of a lost sparrow.

What a story the forest told, and still the beast doubted.

It was not until its mighty feet, more claw than hoof, stretched out along the rough ground that it started to understand, when the hard bone and stony hooks carved deep into solid clay, forming ruts that would never truly be made whole. It closed once more its blackened eyes and opened up its blackened mind. Hunched in the dark of its cave, invisible tendrils cast into earth like roots of a thirsty tree, the beast became part of that cold, murmuring ground.

A beast had need of no sight when every flitting blade of grass, every sway of every tree, every flower lilting in a breeze made its presence known, when the merest tremble of ground flowed into the creature's grasp and unto its control. Everything that walked its forest, from its first step to its last, did so only with the beast's nod.

And for this reason, borne out as immutable truth over countless ages, the beast struggled to accept.

The beating of a heart is a curious thing, fatally fragile yet so full of fire. It is a hidden thing, a guarded thing, a treasure kept from prying eyes and greedy hands. But nothing is withheld from the master of the forest, and when first one flickering pulse, then another and others still, entered its domain, the beast shuddered with the shock of six fluttering heartbeats and the dance of energy that flowed into its grasp. It dug its hooves deep into the earth, twisting and raking and scraping, lusting for the life, insatiable for the taste.

It was then the beast believed, then it knew the truth—men had come, and they had brought their flesh with them, tender offerings to a forgotten god.

The creature leapt to its feet, and the cloudless day began to thunder.

29

The trees had changed, gone rotten somehow, under the skin where the eye couldn't see, as if to take a knife to the bark would draw not sap but bile. Bitch had noticed it, as had Ghost, but he would not be distracted, however much his mother earth tried to warn him of his folly. He gave no second look to the crush of silent wood, the watchful oaks with their leering hollows.

Bitch moved warily, skirting the rough bark, scaly and reptilian to her eyes. The ground beneath her tread had long since lost its solid comfort; the land rose and fell in uneven swells where thick roots drove up damp soil into gathering mounds like the barrows of minor creatures. The deeper their party ventured, the more brooding and threatening the air became, as if an unseen cloud moved among their midst, invading mind and spirit both until the party's thoughts became as dark as their task.

They reached the cave by mid-morning. Ghost had led them, his swiftness of foot all the more shaming for his grievous injuries. The hardy crew behind could scarcely match his dogged pace, but their pale tracker had a vengeance on his mind that would not be put off even one stray moment.

The stone formation showed nothing extraordinary—a rise of dirt and the rocky access that led into the dour earth. Yet how sinister a place it seemed to them then, they whose minds had been poisoned by doubt, plagued by an uncertain fear that had taken root the evening before and was only then coming to fruition. The beast's shrill cry still echoed within them, the unending roar that threatened to snuff out reason and sanity. Bitch and Patch and Ghost had each looked upon the living source of the thunder—Ghost more closely than he cared to recall. The fell knowledge should have driven them running when it only drove them onward.

Their weapons had been drawn well before the cave mouth had come into sight—back when the lightless gulf that demarcated worlds known and worlds apart was still a thing merely felt, if not yet seen. Ghost knew where he walked; he had taken them to the very doorstep of the beast, and he had done so without any of them being discovered, for there was nothing in the air that resembled the horrid cries or the thunderous feet.

In fact, there was nothing in the air at all. Neither wind nor bird stirred the ether that afternoon. It should have been a warning.

Sturmund gathered them close, waiting for Ghost to join. The pale companion had lingered, strange eyes lost to the forest, neither the cave nor the group the object of his focus, but the land itself and its odd, rutted hide. Only Sturmund's beckon drew him away from whatever was troubling him.

"We hold it in its den," Sturmund said after examining

the structure before them and gambling much on there being only one entrance. "We do not let it run."

There was silence, a scuff of boot, then someone cleared his throat.

"Something to say, Scholar?" The familiar weariness clouded Sturmund's brow, but no sooner had it alighted than the great man shook it free. He would not be denied his day, even if it meant parting ways with those whose company he had come to value.

Marney dug at his scalp with a restless finger. "Something about foxes and corners, Captain." Sturmund's eyes narrowed ominously, and Marney finished hastily. "But the precise details elude me at present. Carry on, sir."

"That is our approach," Sturmund said, perhaps more forcefully than intended. "I will lead us in." This last, coming as not a little disappointing to Culp, who had been eyeing the foreboding cavern as an explorer with a claim to stake. "And together," Sturmund said for Culp's benefit, "we earn our glory."

If not by word then by expression, Sturmund's men made their reservations known. Where Culp and Ghost were merely impatient, Bitch's eyes, so rarely downcast, saw only the ground beneath her Captain's feet. Patch grinned away as if there were no more ridiculous creatures under the sky than his brothers-in-arms.

"You as well, Patch?" Sturmund would hear his men, one and all, even if their words would find only deaf ears.

"I was just wondering, Captain, what gave you the impression this creature has designs on running?" The grin grew wider, the man apparently well pleased with what could possibly be his last words on the earth.

Sturmund did something then that none of them expected, something none of them had ever seen, and it took aback the entire party, flippant rogue included: he smiled.

"There are no tougher warriors on this earth," Sturmund said, beaming truly, if uncannily. "If this beast has sense, when it meets you, me, all of us," he said, opening his arms, "it will run for its sorry life."

There were no more complaints after that, even Patch walking tall as they marched into the cave. Ghost paused only a moment at the dark mouth, glancing back to the rutted land with worry and doubt, before his white form disappeared into blackness.

30

As soon as the warriors passed beneath the shadow of the rocks, parched mouths began to water, stale saliva pooling sourly. All of them spat, curses and spittle both streaming from revolted lips. They would have sooner parted with their tongues than taste a moment longer the breath of that fetid cavern.

Patch laughed. There was nothing mirthful about the soulless chuckle. He simply knew no other way to react to something so foul. The rancid putrefaction in the air overwhelmed them, even Sturmund lowering his guard a moment to wipe at bleary eyes.

"Gods," Patch said, "that is lewd."

It was death that hung in the air, a most familiar companion to them all. But it was not merely the death of flesh that haunted the cavern, but the death of the years themselves. Sealed up in that damp enclosure where neither light nor air could breed, in such climes where all else perished, madness thrived. The infernal stench drove them on to their tasks with renewed vigor.

The search did not take long—one primary chamber no

bigger than their own encampment and a few meandering crevices, most too narrow for either beast or man to probe.

"No," Sturmund said, his sword alone still held aloft. "It must be here."

The group watched as their Captain scoured the corners of the chamber, darting suddenly down alcoves only to return a moment later, distressed by the dead end he had encountered.

"There must be more tunnels," he said, a frayed note in the voice disturbing one and all. "Look around, all of you."

And they did, and they found nothing. He was their Captain. When he told them to do something, they did it, and when the time was right, they would speak.

"Where is it?" Sturmund asked, turning suddenly on Ghost, whose calm features never cracked even as those around him tensed. "You led us here. Where is my beast?"

Ignoring the Captain's telling slip of the tongue in a way Patch never would have been able, Ghost merely offered up his professional assessment of their situation.

"This is its larder, not its lair," the pale tracker said, soft voice echoing strangely in the hollowness. "It feeds here. It does not live here. I see that now."

"Doesn't shit where it eats," Patch offered, unhelpfully.

"It brought me here to feed. I escaped. It has no reason to return."

"Where is it?"

There was something terrible in the way Sturmund spoke, something dark and unnerving, and it seemed to them all as if the cavern and its sickly fumes had infected their Captain's mind.

But it had done nothing of the kind. What lay within Sturmund had been there always, just as within the beast had always been the hunger. Ghost knew this, could see it clearly in the cold, blue eyes.

"Answer me," their Captain demanded, "where is my beast?" His raised voice splintered against the cavern walls and rebounded down the myriad crevices, his single frantic voice returning to the group fractured and desperate.

"Somewhere else," the pale man said, and walked out of the cave, hoping greatly that his Captain would follow him back into the light.

Sturmund did not follow; neither did the others.

There was gold in the abandoned cave, heaps and layers of hammered silver, glinting gem, and polished coin. Under centuries of bone and sin lay the treasure of the ages. All that was wanting was the hand, the first to lay down arms to gather up the spoils.

Culp eyed the boneyard with distaste, Marney never giving it a look at all. Bitch had eyes only for her Captain, leaving Patch to covet for them all.

Down to his knees, the one-eyed man fell, half-blind in light, all-blind in the dark. He scraped and scooped, tossing aside carcass and bone for snatches of gold and silver both. His satchel filled quickly and on the ground was weightless. But when he slung the strap over his narrow shoulder and made to stand, he wondered a moment whether he had somehow strung the earth itself to the bursting pack.

"Leave it," Bitch said, and the eerie detachment with which she spoke caused the man to look from his efforts.

She wasn't smiling, which was nothing new, though the worry furrowing at her brow was.

Culp and Marney had already made for the forest, casting long and hopeful glances at their Captain as they went. Sturmund had not moved or spoken, half his frame sheathed in shadow, lighting him like a statue that aimed to portray more than the subject's form.

"But," Patch said in his simple way, "gold."

Bitch shook her head, a somber gesture, and Patch watched, confused, as she too took her leave of them.

Two men remained in darkness, prisoners both to shadows. And had not one of them set down his burden, the other might never have escaped.

31

There were many scents on the air that day, meats aging into fine and varied meals. From outside its petty den, the beast scented its prey, never moving as it did, even as the foolish men came so close to where it lay, face down in the dirt, under leaf and earth, another motionless mound in a forest of shallow graves.

The paleskin, the strange-fleshed thing, had seemed to sense something of its presence, though only for a moment, thoughtless fealty diverting what might have saved them all. Now, as the creature sniffed the air, he considered the coming feast.

There was weary flesh, an old man's bones, good for chewing but lacking richness.

Strange flesh there was, a cursed creature's meat, but the beast knew the color of one's hide had nothing to do with the virtue of its flavor.

There was strong flesh, full of brutish grit, tough and meaty if not complex.

Young flesh there was among them, uncommonly tender for all its presumed virility.

And a woman's flesh, a thing in short supply to the beast, only men reckless enough to cut so deep a path into its realm. It lingered on the scent, slaver heavy on its jowls. Damaged, anguished, but wild for all that, with wishful lust and hopeless longing to soften the rigid muscle—it would relish such a meal.

The scent of fatty flesh was missing, and the beast regretted its loss. It would have made flavorful eating. It had proven itself loud of mouth, and the wails it would have made as the beast feasted on its living meat would have been welcome music to its lonely ears.

But there was another. A flesh so rare as the beast believed it may have never tasted. Its memory told it as much, but its bones spoke another tale. If the beast had feasted on flesh such as this, it had been in ages long past, a time of different men, an age of heroes.

A churn of the beast's gut shook the ground in which it hid, and, as the group departed the cave, trickling out unevenly, marching off more slowly than they had come, the beast slowly rose, earth and dry leaves sifting off its hide. It wished to watch a while longer, no harm in savoring scarce pleasures, and on voiceless feet it followed.

32

They did not return to camp. Many longing eyes had glanced the way to fires and open-roads, but tired legs trudged on towards parts unknown and the quarry within.

Marney stumbled painfully over one of the countless patches of uneven ground that dotted the landscape. There was a delicate moment where he looked to fall, his unwieldy pack slipping precariously and taking his balance with it, but until he actually hit the dirt, none was prepared to reach out a hand. The old scholar asked no favors, and the over-generous risked nursing painful lumps for days.

"One day you'll break," Patch said, casually. "Just snap right in two under all that junk."

There was unease among them, something of that foul stench still clinging to their clothes as they left the cave behind. Patch, for all his snide habits, was doing his part to clear the air.

"And one day," Marney said, doing his best to hide his labored breathing, "you'll learn some manners. Both days, I suspect, lie a ways off yet."

Sturmund gave his men a look back over his shoulder,

one that suggested, in the icy stillness of his eyes, that holding one's tongue was infinitely preferable to having it cut off. Patch and Marney both fell to a silence that carried nothing of contrition, each busy thinking on the best possible crack to throw at the other when next they sparred. Until then, on they marched, Patch sliding gracefully through the thicket, his lithe figure producing nothing more than whispers as he moved, while Marney trudged, relentless as a tortoise, with the bulk and heft of his travel chest strapped to his bent frame.

It was the smaller of the scholar's two trunks, often worn, while the other, now stowed safely back at the encampment, required towing. Within its leathery, shell-like hide were crammed all manner of cumbersome references —local histories of town and people, charts and flowing maps folded down to nothing by the old soldier's dexterous handling, instruments of navigation more suited to the open seas than the narrow woods. Ponderous and indispensable —such was the way with knowledge, and Marney bore the burden without complaint.

As they went, Sturmund's second took constant readings with a rusted compass and another strange device he kept staring through with his rheumy eyes. Together, the tools appeared to provide him some sense of bearing, which he excitedly translated to the folded map tucked in his waistband. Ghost watched without comment, his dubious expression censure enough, Marney's careless trampling both offensive and bemusing to the tracker's shining eyes.

The paleskin needed no science to know where he stood. It was art that guided his tracker's feet, every tree a signpost, every patch of dirt unique, all committed to memory, as were the faintest scents and secret songs of the forest, guides and beacons as strong as any magnetic pull, provided one spoke the language. Ghost knew exactly where they were and had been. As it happened, so did Marney. Neither, however, knew quite where their path led—where it ended or what lay upon it. It troubled neither; no man knew such things.

After long and thirsty hours, Sturmund finally stopped, and the silent band did as well, sweating and breathing hard. They had come far, too far to return before nightfall. Their course was set, and it led into darkness.

Sturmund turned, first to Ghost, who, with a quick shake of his head, told his Captain he had not picked up any trace of their prey. Then to Marney, his faithful second, he looked for more precise orientation.

"We're off the map soon enough," the old soldier said, stretching out the many-folded parchment.

Sturmund saw, and said nothing. His cool eyes looked from the faint marking of their camp and along the wavering line etched in Marney's steady hand that charted their current course. They had covered more ground than Ghost and Hull, Patch and Bitch.

The light of day, now darkened with the tired hues of late afternoon, had been good to them, allowing speed which by night would have been impossible. It had also brought them within reach of uncharted territories. The green swath of forest depicted on the scholar's map ended unceremoniously at the upper edge of the parchment, and the current position of their group, marked faintly in ink, lay one small measure below.

"You have no other charts in your stockpile?"

"I have charts aplenty, Captain," Marney said. "But none of them for where we hope to tread."

Sturmund was quiet, his eyes speaking for him. Every one of them could see the troubled thoughts rippling across the blue waters. Ruffled strands of blond hair fell down across his face, spilling over the back of his shoulder and giving their Captain the noble air of an aged lion.

In any group so long united, there is seldom use for words, especially in times when much needed to be communicated quickly. There was a question the Captain needed to put to his men, and after the darkness of the beast's den, the answer stood uncertain. The lion gazed upon its pride.

First to Culp, his strongest, who stood motionless among the fallen leaves. Sturmund turned his eyes and waited. They had shared, perhaps, a dozen words in the years since they joined one another's company, yet Sturmund felt he knew Culp best of all his men. The song of steel, the test of mettle—there are things no words can share, only action. Their eyes met, and whatever passed between the two, passed in stoic silence—whatever Sturmund saw, a comfort to him.

Then to Bitch, his toughest, the Captain turned his rugged gaze. She straightened herself, first resolve, then desire, pulling at her lips as she stared hopefully, longingly, into his eyes. He had little need to ask if she meant to accompany him, though sadly did all the same; for all he saw in her, he never saw deeply enough. She closed her eyes, ready to die for him.

On Ghost's face was the deadly calm. Sturmund knew the pale-faced man would walk into hell if that way led their path, and Sturmund would be glad of such capable company. A nod of the Captain's head; a faint shrug of the tracker's shoulders. The slight of the hours before, in the darkness of the cave, forgiven.

That left Marney, whose wry eyes and grizzled features were a thing almost beautiful to the Captain's soul, for an old soldier is too often a defeated soldier. Marney had never

We Burn Our Dead

broken, never even bent. In all the long years, his faithful second had only grown more fierce, more wise. The blade of Marney's spear could have cut night from day, yet how dull a thing compared to the scholar's mind. Marney knew Sturmund's thoughts as well as his own. They had come far together, and, with one curt nod from his lieutenant, Sturmund rejoiced that they would go farther still.

At last, Patch. Difficult Patch.

Sturmund stared, the moments stretching on. Patch did not seem to notice the tension rising from the men around him.

"What do you think, Patch?" Sturmund spoke uncommonly gently. "Do we go on?"

Patch gave no indication he had heard. He was staring, almost dumbly, at his Captain.

A broken man, Sturmund thought. Not quite whole. But Sturmund knew the pieces were not lost, only misplaced, disarranged.

The stillness grew dangerously heavy, but Sturmund let it hang. He would have waited there until their feet sank into the ground. True things required patience. Sturmund would have gone on alone, but it would not have been right for them to have broken after coming so far along the same worn path; this was a thing meant for them all.

And just as hope of glory seemed lost, their reckless quest overturned, from the blankness of Patch's face, a wicked smile broke.

"Sure," the one-eyed man said, cavalier to the last. "Let's go knock on that monster's door."

Sturmund had his answer—he had not lost his men, he had found his warriors.

The Captain seemed larger to them then, grown before their eyes and minds and hearts. His broad figure swelled with breath and life, his shadow stretched and wide in the steep angles of the late sun. A lion waking.

"You have parchment, Scholar?"

"I'd be a sorry excuse for a learned man if I did not," Marney said, affronted. "And if I'd run out, I'd cut down that bitch of an elm over yonder and scratch my thoughts on its skin."

Sturmund almost smiled. "Good. Then get your finest sheet and sharpest quill. You sketch your own map tonight."

The lion stalked off into the forest, and the pride followed after.

33

It smelled them. On the wind, it tasted them—their scent gamey and rich. *Flesh.* It felt them, their blind, arrogant footsteps leading them the way to pain and darkness.

The beast hungered. Raved. Yearned. Needed.

And before the day was out, it would *have*.

34

The beast, it seemed, could move without trace, if it so wished. More often though, like any cur greedy of its territory, the beast chose to leave its mark, the sudden and mindless ruin they now encountered clear proof of its infrequent restraint.

They journeyed well into the night, their path as bleak as their prospects for rest. The desolation of the beast stretched miles, had felled countless trees and tilled the hard earth into ruts of loose soil as far as the eye could trace. They needed no trackers where they were going. The beast hid nothing of its passage, the thought of any creature seeking it out perhaps never once having crossed its feral mind.

So on came the warriors, silent and grave, six dark shapes moving as one, eyes blind in the heavy night as they trudged their way along, thoughts bent on the same simple goal—destruction of the beast, revenge for their fallen brother, reclamation of their tarnished pride. The way proved difficult, with more than darkness to obscure their path.

A forest has many voices, from the whispered hush of gold-lit afternoons to the icy hiss of wintry evenings, the pensive groans of the ruminating wood to the threatening cracks of the withered tree. A forest, then, is like a riddle, speaking with countless tongues, where every leaf tells a tale, the endless murmur of trees a meaningless babel to the uninitiated.

No language of the wild was unknown to the man called Ghost, who knew every call of winged bird, every cry of woodland creature—the great symphony of forest life, a harmony of countless small parts. He carried this knowledge with him as he moved ahead of the pack, point-man for his brothers, Marney's eyes too weak to read the stars or see his own scratches on the dim parchment. All looked to Ghost to lead them through impenetrable night, the pooling shadows almost palpable, hands instinctively reaching out as they walked as if to part a dark veil before their eyes. The responsibility was great, and Ghost bore it gravely, which was why his failure hurt so keenly.

Three blind hours into their grueling trek, Ghost stopped, the rest of the weary band halting abruptly when they realized their guide had fallen still. No one spoke, all eyes on the tracker, his pale skin a faint glow in the darkness ahead. Ghost was glad of their feeble sight. He would have shamed for anyone to see the worry creasing at his brow, the habitual calm so long enjoyed, so much admired, now, so easily shattered—and by nothing.

Nothing. That was what had undone the mysterious tracker, the silent hunter, the sphinx-like Ghost. He stood with his back to the rest, not ready to face them, unsure even if he could. Since Marney had announced with ill-considered delight their departure from *terra nota*, quill tracing rapidly and adeptly the novel contours of the nameless forest, Ghost had been struck as if by fever, all his senses rendered useless.

He had pressed on boldly for the past few hours, but reckless confidence stepped quickly aside for racing dread. His ears rang with the ugly throb of silence, the forest coldly mute. There was nothing to hear—no wind through tree branch, no scuttle of furtive animal, nothing. The forest would not speak to him, and for the first time in his life, Ghost felt alone.

Never one for the company of others, his kinship with the wilds had been all that had sustained him through the lonely years. And to be now so unexpectedly abandoned—it cut him more deeply than any fang ever could. Once more, Ghost had found himself an orphan.

Marney drew nearer, his clumsy tread unpleasantly pronounced in the sudden vacuum of the night, the unceremonious drop of his trunk an insult to Ghost's raw senses—every movement, every breath of human making only accentuated the greater loss he felt.

"What is it?" Marney asked, his voice a deafening whisper to the tracker's starving ears. "What do you see?"

Behind the two, the unsheathing hiss of steel cut through the silent air like a knot of serpents. They could not see their brother, but all had sense enough that something was amiss. Ghost did not stop unless he absolutely had to, and he never made them wait.

Ghost seemed a long time turning, and when Marney saw the worry spilling out of those violet eyes, he looked at once to Sturmund.

"Something's wrong," Marney hissed, and down the line, each man readied for trouble.

"What is it, Ghost?" Sturmund had joined the pair, and now Captain and lieutenant tried to make sense of the inexplicable collapse of the man each had thought unbreakable.

Ghost shook his head, his wild, brilliant eyes darting through the darkness around them as if at any moment the beast might leap forth. Sturmund did not require anything more.

"On me," said the Captain to his men.

If the command came simply, the effect was immediate and powerful. Four swift figures encircled Sturmund and Ghost, weapons drawn, bodies turned to confront the leering night. Bitch, Patch, Culp, and Marney took up their positions, one quarter of the world each theirs to defend.

"It's here." A wild, wild fear wrapped Ghost's words.

Sturmund gripped the back of Ghost's head and brought it close to his own, shining eyes meeting cold stare.

"Can you breathe?" the Captain asked.

"It's been here all along." Ghost's eyes flickered. A quick, nervous glance shot over Sturmund's broad shoulder before falling back on the blue gaze of the warrior-king.

"Can you breathe?" repeated his Captain, his callused hand a vice on the back of Ghost's sweat-slicked head. Only one answer would do.

Ghost nodded haltingly, breathing deep, steadiness returning.

The corner of Sturmund's mouth gave an almost imperceptible upward tug. He pressed his forehead against Ghost's, feeling the anxious sweat against his hot brow.

"Then let us make our stand." And to the group, Sturmund gave the order.

The four sentinels stepped two silent paces forward, their perimeter widening, the lethal compass growing by two points. Sturmund took position between Bitch and Patch, Ghost between Culp and Marney. Around the six, the night began to squeeze, black as pitch, heavy as the darkest sea. A single arm's length all that separated each link of their chain—still, the night did much to swallow one from view of another.

"Nothing will break us," Sturmund said, his voice profound, and to Ghost, the first sound that stood a chance of filling the foul silence brooding in the air.

They waited, arms gleaming, breath steaming, muscles tensed and poised. The darkness swirled, tightened, closed ranks. And for a while, a stalemate seemed in the offing, neither party giving ground to the other, the wicked night kept at bay by sheer force of will, the fearsome band held immobile by waves of crushing black.

It is no small thing to hold a steady guard, the solid heft of cutting steel sapping constantly a man's strength. Culp's mighty blade weighed heavily, yet it remained stone-still in his powerful hands, raised high to defend his brothers, raised high to deliver a punishing blow.

The ready draw of a bow string requires less strength than a two-handed sword, but the endurance to hold it taut would test the burliest of fighter's resolve. Patch appeared frozen in time, the arrow knocked to his bowstring a study in deadly potential.

So it was with all Sturmund's warriors, their control of arms no less masterly than their employment of them. Yet time has a way of catching all things in its snare. However fleet of foot or mindful of eye, in the end, time's inevitable shoulder-tap catches every man unaware.

Marney took a faint sniff through his nose, a stolen breath that alerted everyone to his condition. The spear tip extended motionlessly into the night, the heavy haft tucked under lean arm pinned by iron muscles. Yet iron, as anyone who wields such crude tools knows, rusts.

"Keep it together, old man," Patch whispered, striking up their long-overdue argument.

Marney tightened his abdomen and hugged the haft more firmly to his aching side. The tremble of spear tip subsided, but Marney knew not for how long.

"You just mind that string, laddie," Marney said of the taut bowstring at Patch's cheekbone. "Wouldn't want you accidentally losing the good one. What a pleasure to be around you'd be then."

"Quiet," Bitch said, expecting nothing of the sort.

It is the peculiar trait of the warrior to quip in times of greatest stress. In the thick of battle or the beast-stalked night, the warrior could always be counted on to let off steam with idle chatter. What was good for morale was good for the fight. That was why Sturmund ignored them.

Silence resumed for another brief interval, during which each warrior remained at painful vigilance. Patch's bowstring had not quivered any more than it had when Marney had first joked, yet the tremble in the old soldier's spear had increased markedly.

The minutes ticked passed. Patch rolled his eye. Patience, above all other virtues, was a thing the young man was loathe to practice.

"Ghost," Patch said, a little too loudly, "are you sure it's even around here, or are we just being assholes?"

No answer. Ghost was behind him, eyes lost in the haze of night, ears burning at the treachery of the still air.

"Ghost," Patch called again, "I don't think this thing's even—"

"Will you just shut—" Marney had lost his temper. Worse, he had lost his focus. He never finished the thought.

The spear dipped, only for an instant, tipping towards the sullen earth when it should have been raised, always above center, ready to repel at a moment's notice the advance of enemy forces.

The dip of the spear, the slight turn of his head, the dismissive grin he loved to offer Patch—even the smallest things have weight. Like the momentary flit of his iron gaze—that mistake, next to heaps of gold, weighed most of all, and cost Marney just as dearly.

The shadows erupted, rent like tissue by the shrewd beast, which all that time had lain perched just out of sight, stony hooves flexed in darkness even as the warrior's weapons stood readied. Only this beast cared nothing of time, living outside its nagging current, unaffected by the erosion of the years. Its waiting was eternal, its wrath absolute, its victory certain. As inevitable as the coming dawn was its violence—a simple matter of when.

On powerful hind legs the beast launched itself into the air, moving more silently than silence, the sight of the creature in its flight ghastly in its unnatural grace, horrid in its sickly quiet.

Marney did nothing, which was precisely all he could have done. He gaped at the massive form sailing through the air and covering more distance in the single leap than seemed possible. As the beast came, its jaws began to open, and continued to open all the while, stretching beyond the point where ligaments must surely contain the muscles, a vast, yawning, impossible chasm of glinting teeth, jagged razors, hungry dark. And into that darkness the scholar went, his parchment tucked into his belt, an unfinished map to lead him through the nightmare.

SPEAR SONG

Days grow short in the winter months, when hope flies south on hurried wing, when spirits sink and hearts grow heavy and dull—with scarcely a warning, evening had stretched its languid arms around the outpost and drawn tight its grip. Even from the higher reaches of the settlement, little could be made anymore of the surrounding fields and still less of the treeline beyond, now but a denser streak of black across the shadowed canvass. Twin rows of torches extended down from the barred gates into the open night, where they flickered like pinprick stars adrift in ocean darkness. God or demon might have stalked the burned-out fields, but none of the watch would be any the wiser for it.

Weary sentinels had watched crimson skies succumb to leaden cloud, had seen a wan, wolfish moon usurp a once-brilliant seat. Under such weighty gloom, tired minds often flee to furthest despair. For the men of the watch, it appeared as though the world they had known by day—broad, brimming, bright—had simply laid down arms and skulked away, leaving them and their outpost the lone remaining refuge against an ever-deepening dark. Silent watchmen cursed the traitorous day, even as they longed for its return.

Fear rose like bile in the throat, and no cider could mask the bitter taste. Dread crept on spindly legs, and no shake of cloak would dislodge its needling clasp.

In the blind distance, an animal called, its wretched cry a pang to the stillness. It was alone in the darkness, this lost lamb, more alone than it realized. It could not bear to pass the night with only shadows for company. The sentries knew the folly of such desperate need; it did not do to attract attention when there was none to watch one's back.

A moment later, the cry cut short, and as silence returned, heavy hearts sank lower still.

A chill wind whistled through the battlements; the rough slats of timber, all that held the terrors of a hungry world at bay, clattered where they had been ineptly secured. The din was ceaseless on the wall, and the din was welcome. For though it may have grated the nerves, it also distracted the worried heart—if only for a time.

"I'm to report to the watch commander." The figure stood like stone on the narrow ramparts, eyes forward, wind catching the dark strands at his temples, as he waited to be recognized.

The officer took a step back from where he leaned at the wall. He had been squinting up at the sky, searching for the stars he felt sure must be there. Dark clouds glided overhead, coveting the glittering lights from the needful eyes of men.

He had not heard the man approach, and only exhaustion had kept him from making his surprise known. As it was, he merely turned a tired face to meet the newcomer; he was unprepared for what he found.

The officer knew a soldier when he saw one; the sight was rare enough as to be damned miraculous. Pig-farmers and half-wits—that was what he had been forced to make due with. The governor would not spend precious coin to recruit decent men, fighting men, and insisted that they make do with the villagers—that was what had gotten them into the mess in the first place.

"Our new recruit," the officer said, trying to mask the many strong emotions he felt pressing at his over-tired breast. Relief. Resentment. Fear. "You came in with the morning, I hear—down from the Northern routes, of all places."

The soldier said nothing.

"Strange you should come to us from such a place." The officer nodded to the darkness, but meant the now-hidden Northern trail, which cut through forest and over hill, bypassed civilization at every turn, skirted even the most remote encampment, until it let its travelers out at the god-forsaken stretch of dirt and death on which the outpost had been hastily erected.

The soldier said nothing. In fact, if the officer hadn't know any better, he would have said the man actually managed to say even less. He pressed him further, frustration if not good sense urging him on.

"Nothing that way except long miles and harder trail. In fact, last thing to come down from there were the same wretched sorts that have us manning the walls tonight." There was a challenge in the words.

The soldier's silence had grown deadly.

"You didn't happen to see anyone along the way," the officer asked, "did you?"

"I saw no one," the soldier said. There was no resentment in the answer, which gave the officer strength, however fragile, to continue.

"What brings you here?"

"My reasons are my own." Simple as that. A soldier alright.

"Must be something awful leads a Northman south. Must be something worse causes him to sign up with this sorry lot." The officer might have been speaking of the newcomer; he might have been speaking of them both.

"I was passing. My purse is running light." Money. Always money. "I was told you needed men to guard your walls. I hear you have a problem. Unwanted guests."

The officer made an ugly face, giving a glance over the wall, to what he hoped were empty shadows below. Dropping the subject of the soldier's unlikely arrival, he turned to something altogether more unkind.

"Damned bad business," the officer said, rubbing the rough stubble at his chin. "First was bandits. That was bad. Killed a score of townsfolk. Workman's guild pressed the governor into hiring mercenaries." He paused, perhaps reflecting. "That was worse."

The soldier raised an eyebrow. "They take care of your bandit problem?"

"That would be putting it mildly. You should have heard the sounds that came out of the forest that night." The officer had turned his back on the fields completely, not wishing to set eyes on the sight lest the memories return too vividly. Fear, however, continued to loosen his tongue. "Bunch of devils. Didn't seem so bad when we were paying them."

"What happened?"

"What always happens that makes men die. Governor

got greedy. Held out on what we owed them. Should have known the fat prick was up to something when he shelled out the promise of coin so easily." Here the officer spat, a greasy phlegm he lobbed over the wall. "He had no intention of paying them. Now the bastards say we have 'till tonight to reconsider our position."

Here the officer spat again, but the effect was one much diminished. Some of the spittle caught on his lip and ran down his chin. He wiped it away with the back of his hand, and ran the hand across his breeches.

"You have my spear," the soldier said, "through the night."

The stoic words calmed the officer some, reminded him of their positions, their duties.

"What's your name, soldier?"

"Marney," the soldier said, watching the officer carefully.

"Marney, eh? Old name." The officer fell thoughtful, scratching the patch of his chin once more. "Seems I may have heard it before." Another moment passed. "You serve with the King's army?"

"Once." There was no mistaking the finality in the word. The conversation was at an end. The officer was not offended.

Perhaps the soldier really was the traveler he claimed to be. Perhaps simple chance had led him down the trails just behind the mercenaries. The officer did not know. All he knew was the soldier looked an honest man, and if trusting him proved to be the last mistake the officer ever made, he would die without much regret, knowing as he did that one way or another, Death was coming to the walls that night.

"How many?" Marney had taken up beside the officer and begun scanning the fields below.

The officer shrugged. "At least three. Likely more."

"Three?" Marney furrowed his brow. There had to have been ten guards standing sentry along various points of the walls, with just as many walking the grounds or loitering in the barracks. All this for three men?

The officer offered a mirthless smile. "You didn't see them. Their eyes," he said, "they were like . . . like nothing I have known."

"Full of fire?" Marney asked. He had begun to doubt. A gull might seem a dragon to one who has never looked to the sky. So it was with men who have never known true battle, when a first foe seems always like the last foe one will ever face.

"No fire." The officer's voice had grown small, drawn inward. "No anything. Just . . . hollow."

"Three men," Marney said again, more to himself now. And he set himself to a closer inspection of the fields, leaning over the wall, wrapping his hands on the lip of the battlements, embracing the rough, splintered edge and drawing himself further across to better see the grounds.

A ring of torches illuminated the perimeter of the outpost, the warding, yellow light like a sick-house glow, telling travelers to pass on, that only death was to be found within. A few feet from the walls and the light faded to a paltry haze, a shadowed border between terrors known and those yet to be revealed, both dreadful in their respective manner. Any further from the walls was to enter the dominion of night, its utter blackness perfectly silent, profoundly still, undeniably alive.

The gates, thirty feet below, lay almost directly underfoot of officer and soldier, and a strange magnetism drew Marney's attention back from the darkness and towards the vacant spot of ground before the shut and barred entry. It is there that his eyes lingered longest.

We Burn Our Dead

There are places on the earth—occasionally, in the earth—that are nevertheless, not of the earth. Though comprised of the same mean elements that form the remainder of all existence, these places are marked for purpose greater than their humble parts might suggest, and therefore exist apart, waiting for a moment as set by fate. It is in that waiting that such places acquire strength, are often given reverence—some are set aside as shrines and holy grounds; more are merely avoided by idle foot and careless eye, skirted and left to bide. Marney had no doubt that the entry to the outpost, a paltry patch of trodden dirt, was one such place. His eyes saw not dead earth and lifeless clay, but the living, breathing skin of the world, a timeless skein, a strange stage set and readied for the nameless actor.

"One was as broad as the gate," the officer said, calling Marney back from a peculiar train of thought, though leaving his eyes to wonder still. "Hair like fire, a beard of searing embers." The officer recalled the image and troubled himself by doing so.

Marney paid the talk little mind. It did not do to indulge fancy.

"Another, he moved like death—slow and perfectly sure." The officer paused. "Wild eyes."

"And the third?" Despite Marney's best efforts, grim curiosity had taken hold. The claws sunk deep. At last he found the strength to take his eyes from the field below. Only for an instant.

The officer swallowed. "Their leader," he said. "He was—"

Three hard knocks sounded against the rough wood of the gate; three heavy blows that made the ponderous timber ring hollow.

"The hell is at the gate?" The officer had roused himself

on the instant, all campfire tales cast aside in the face of grimmer reality. "Weren't you watching?"

He lunged towards the wall, shoving Marney aside.

Of course Marney had been watching, as had half a dozen other men their side of the catwalk, each of whom now peered hesitantly over the battlements, one as surprised as the next to spy the lone figure standing before the gate. Only Marney failed to register surprise; he felt only odd relief.

"It's a demon." The call came from a man of the watch, who now raced across from his post, not wishing to pass the moment alone. Marney saw he was scarcely yet a man, and hardly a soldier. Then the smell caught up with him, and Marney placed it instantly; the boy was a pig-farmer.

"Shut your mouth," the officer snapped, his eyes never leaving the figure at the gate.

The pig-farmer whispered, and continued to whisper for some minutes: "A demon come to take us all."

Marney frowned at the boy, but found the sentiment hard to argue with. There was a decidedly otherworldly aspect to the figure below, standing so fixedly to that fateful plot of ground, as though he could have waited forever for reply, as though he had not just marched up to the gates of a fortified position.

But, of course, he had not marched. He had appeared.

That must be what the loneliest man in the world looks like, Marney thought. He had to get a closer look.

Marney was already halfway down the ladder before the officer managed to bark the order.

"Secure that gate. Let no one pass."

When he reached the courtyard, there were already two footmen before the mouth of the gate, their trembling spears pointed uselessly at the shut portal.

Before he could stand them aside, Marney heard the officer coming up behind him.

"By me, soldier," he said, a hoarse whisper to Marney as he passed. A moment later and he was at the gate, Marney right with him.

The officer reached out a hand, and a drew back a sliver of wood to make way for a glimpse of the night beyond their walls. Through the slot, Marney saw the eyes, cold and searing, fiery and glacial. Occasional plumes of breath steamed in the air and hid the gaze from view, only for it to return a moment later just as intense.

"I am come for my payment."

Perhaps only the confidence in the bulk of dense timber separating their two positions gave the officer strength enough to reply. The rest of his men did not seem to share their commander's faith in the sturdiness of the walls and began to inch away slowly.

"The governor refuses your payment."

The mercenary made no sign of comprehension. He stood unmoved, and seemed to be waiting for a more favorable return.

"Had I the gold," the officer rasped, biting his lip as he did so, "I'd pay you myself."

"I do not seek your gold, watchman. I seek my payment."

Marney watched the conversation unfold, at times marveling at the intensity of blue eyes coming through the aperture; at others, trying to figure how the killer on the other side of the gate planned to reclaim his due. Marney knew something more than most about scaling walls, and sensed deception. The conversation between officer and mercenary faded to a low hum as his mind drifted.

"I can't do anything for you." The officer's words droned on.

"My gold." Deep, strong, calm.

"The governor has shut himself up in the—" Barely audible.

"*It is you.*" Clear. Firm. Cutting.

The world is seldom gentle when it grips a man's attention. Marney had been scanning the walls above for any sign of grapples when the sharp words called him back. He realized with a start that the officer was no longer the object of the eyes' focus. If Marney had not known any better, he might have said it was not the stranger's gaze that had shifted onto him, but the earth itself that had turned traitorous, carrying Marney into view of the man.

"It is you," the figure repeated.

"I?" Marney

"You." The somber voice carried softly, the figure speaking perhaps only to himself.

"You know him?" the lieutenant snapped, his earlier suspicions all but confirmed, as he drew a step away from the soldier beside him and placed a firm hand on his hilt.

"I don't—" Marney said, hesitating, shaking his head.

"You were with us. On the ship. All those years ago."

"I can't—" Marney's eyes widened slowly.

"Strange fates bring us together," the figure said, almost reverently. Then, adding in graver tones, "Grant me entry, and you shall see tomorrow. I offer you the same advice you once gave to me: *There is no shame in being wise.*"

And Marney recalled the youth and the rawhide bit offered in kindness.

"I have taken their coin," Marney said, as though all the rest of the confounded watchmen had ceased to exist, that only he and this strange acquaintance were there to consort that evening. "How can I betray that charge?"

The blue eyes did not waver, but Marney sensed a change in their waters.

"Honor," the figure said. "It is rare."

Marney nodded knowingly.

"You would not deny that I have been wronged."

Marney shook his head.

"The governor's life is due along with my coin."

Marney hesitated, nodded.

"Wait just a moment—" The officer, who had for the time followed the conversation as though transfixed, now seemed to rouse from his stupor.

"Only those who stand against us will fall." The words were not compromise, merely reconsideration. They came more quickly than all those that had come before. Marney understood the urgency, and made at once to unbar the gate.

"Wait," the officer said, confusion clouding his course of action, sensing as he did that the soldier had just bartered away the outpost, while still holding onto a chance for them all to survive. "We can't just—"

Marney's hands sprang for the bolt. A not unfamiliar emotion pricked his skin—he had thrown the dice, cast the bones, wagered it all in one daring sweep. How many times before had he gambled as much and won? How many times had he grabbed up his winnings—the very skin on his back—and laughed at his reckless bravery, thence called cunning? More than most was the answer. What he knew for certain was that each victory cut the odds of the next; he never let the knowledge bother him overlong.

"Hold that man." The cry came crashing through the still night air, a voice pregnant with anxiety, wild with fear, simmering with anger, but brimming with profound and undeniable authority.

The governor had emerged from the security of his quarters, and was even then huffing across the courtyard. His commands, lobbed so well in advance of himself, had hit their mark. Three pairs of arms encircled Marney and restrained him not a moment too soon. The bolt clattered back against the wood, its charge still secure.

The blue eyes had disappeared from the aperture, leaving in their place only flickers of soft light thrown by the torches, and a sullen whistle of air.

"Traitorous dog," the governor said, arriving in time to drive a boot into Marney's shin. "And you," the portly man snapped, turning on the officer, "let a cur into my fortress, when he is so clearly just another of those murderous scum."

The officer's eyes scowled, even as his tongue offered up apologies. The relationship between those who wield power and those who merely carry it out was as delicate as it was perverse.

"You'll kill everyone, then?" Marney had been restrained, not gagged, leaving his most dangerous weapon still unsheathed.

The governor cast a baleful glance. "In the morning, you hang."

"Make those gallows wide, governor. You hang with me."

A hard slap followed the ugly grimace, and Marney felt the full weight of the governor's corpulence behind it.

"You all will hang." Marney spat words and blood both, and caught the ear of worried men, some gathered near the gate, others standing like statues upon the dark battlements. "If you're lucky. Who's to say how they'll pay back your hospitality?"

"Shut him up." The governor made an insolent gesture, a petulant sweep of the hand, but was so comfortable in his authority, did not glance to ensure his instructions had been followed.

Marney continued, as the crowd listened.

"I said shut—"

"You hired these men." Marney's voice came down like judgment upon the guards and their governor, upon the bones of the desolate outpost. "And they did the task prescribed, did what none of you could or dared to do. You invited them in, fed them with your promise, asked them to go and brave the dangers of the very night you all can scarcely look upon without shitting yourselves. And this is how you repay such service?"

Even the governor blanched some under the heavy charge. His officer spat once more, this time hitting the polished leather of the governor's boot.

"If your sense of honor does not urge you on to some better course," Marney said, his voice softening, "surely some sense of self-preservation must, for neither man nor wall can keep out what comes for us in the end."

The hands had long since relinquished their hold over the soldier, who now stood of his own free will before the gathered men, his oration done, his wind spent. He cast a glance at the officer, whose face burned with shame. To the man's credit, he did not shy from Marney's gaze, but took the brunt of the stare, like a man should do. The governor was less forthcoming, his brow sweaty, his beady eyes dropping under the soldier's stare. It seemed as though words had won the day. The governor said nothing as Marney turned for the door, and not a man moved to stop him.

Marney approached the gate, the blue eyes still absent from the slot. He had no doubt the man had heard his words; he wondered only if they had mattered, if they had worth. He believed he knew something of the warrior on the other side of the gate; now, reaching for the bolt, Marney intended to discover if he were correct.

There was a movement both behind and before the soldier. A scuff of foot clipped the gravel behind him; the sudden reappearance of eyes filled the aperture before him. The warning in the blue eyes relieved one of Marney's worries, even as it gave rise to still another.

The path of the warrior is only one of many roads the fates have seen fit to lay before our feet. There are paths for heroes and paths for common men, ways to glory and ways to quiet, unremarkable lives. Each road exacts a toll, its fare of passage.

The governor chose none of these routes—not hero, not commoner, being neither himself. He walked instead the way that cowards must, stepping from behind, greeting only the back of Marney's head, before passing the length of spear-tip through the soldier's neck.

Marney fell, but not before his hand had driven the bolt to the furthest reaches of its catch. Even before his body struck the earth, the gate swung free.

The figure that forced its way into the courtyard strode in on graceful legs, with powerful shoulders shrugging off the few hands that thought to reach for him. Marney lost sight of the blond warrior after he stepped over his fallen body. All that Marney could do was bleed-out and listen.

"I am govern—" The inconsolable voice cut short with a grunt of pain, a cry, and a whimper.

A few exchanges of steel rang out in bursts familiar to Marney's ears. He knew the melody so well, this old-familiar song, that it was as if he could see the unseen parries, the feint and slide of cunning blade, the deft plunge of sword into flesh, until finally the dance ended, almost as quickly as it had begun.

"Stand down!" The officer's voice pleaded for reason in the mad moments. "Lay down your arms, you damned fools!"

Whether the words or the warrior quelled the riled hearts, silence fell a moment later. Occasional groaning, soft weeping, broke the emptiness, but somehow made the night seem more hollow still. One of the watch had ducked to Marney's side and taken stock of his wound; the look on his face did not inspire Marney to hope, but the man tended to him no less dutifully. If nothing else, Marney found the unmistakable odor of hay and manure emanating from the man curiously soothing.

Marney faded, his world blurring. A lover of all good tales, he wished to know how this story ended, and hated to think his own would come to a close before the night's events were over. He reached deep and tried to hold on, if only a little longer.

"Bob. Sinner."

Marney did not understand the command the warrior had given, but a clarifying remark from the officer added the necessary context.

"You had—" The officer's disbelief came accompanied by the creak of board high up in the battlements. A watchman cried out in alarm, but no steel sounded. Someone had begun to descend from the wall. "You had men inside?"

"Demon!" Marney heard the pig-farmer lend his own surprise, as another scuff of boot carried down from the opposite catwalk. A second black-clad figure had begun sliding down the ladder.

"I wished to see if there were any worthy men among you. I doubted, but I see now I was wrong to do so."

Dirt crunched as footsteps neared. The figure loomed

over the fallen soldier, his presence casting far further than his shadow.

"Your words this night," the warrior said, "were wise indeed. That is twice now."

The watchman tending to Marney's throat, staunching the blood as best he could, froze in the shadow of the warrior. Marney could only grunt to encourage the medic back to his task.

As the warrior stared down at him, blue eyes offering no comfort, no charity, two black-clad figures, descended now from the battlements, appeared by his side. Marney did not know if it were the delirium of blood loss, but he did not like one bit the madness he saw dancing in their eyes. The odd trio stared down upon him, as even then, a fourth, arriving from outside the outpost walls, made his presence known with loud grunts of exertion and terribly labored breathing.

"I got here . . . as fast . . . as I could." The huge red figure filled the gateway, chest heaving from the effort, enormous hammer raised in one meaty hand. "As soon as . . . I saw the gate . . . open."

The massive figure leaned against the frame of the gateway and stared around at the littered dead and the cowering living. He seemed to be eyeing a few of the terrified watchmen.

"Are these . . . all spoken fer then?" He asked, his hammer obviously itching for a taste.

"We're done here," the warrior said, quite simply, and his two crazed-eyed companions started for the door, much to the protest of the great red brute.

"Can't I just—"

"No," said one of the black-clad duo, edging the Red back into the night.

"How about just a—"

"No," said the other of the odd pair, succeeding in driving the brute scurrying back into the night, and with only a glance of his wild eyes. Marney could hear the grudging tread for some time.

"You have a place with us," the warrior said, who had not taken his eyes from the bleeding soldier before him, "should you wish. If you recover, you need only seek us out."

With the offer made, the blue-eyed warrior, with not so much as a look back on the ruined courtyard, strode out the open gate.

Marney watched him go, consciousness slipping towards the black, a crease at the corners of his eyes.

"I thought you'd . . ." Marney coughed, clotting blood still gurgling in his throat. The voice rose again, fainter than the whispered wind, speaking a secret kept for long years, ". . . never ask."

35

True nightmares are not what troubled minds fall asleep to find; they are what hopeful hearts wake to see sitting at their morning bedside, having waited all along.

Having had the dubious advantage of watching the beast mount its vicious assault, Culp and Patch were among the first to react; they were rewarded little for their efforts. Culp's heavy sword landed only a glancing blow against the indifferent hide, Patch's arrow deflected impotently by the same armored skin. Sturmund, Bitch, and Ghost each turned swiftly enough, and, readied as they were for a fight, were equally unprepared for what actually awaited them.

Marney was gone, taken whole by the beast, which landed within their midst with earthshaking power. The force of the crashing monster dropped Bitch, who fought from the ground with strength undiminished, daggers flying from her skillful hands.

A spray of dark blood surged from the beast's mouth as its dripping jaws closed, sealing Marney forever within. The crimson gore struck Patch full in his face, blinding his lonesome eye and rendering him a dangerous flail of arms and daggers until his sight was restored.

Culp and Sturmund lashed out with heavy blows, the clang of useless steel dull and heavy in the air, the sudden repulse of recoiling blades staggering both men. The beast danced wickedly in their midst, legs kicking, jaws snapping, as the warriors closed ranks around it.

Ghost chanced a single thrust, a timely lunge, well-aimed to the side of the quivering throat. A single scratch of the beast's glistening hide was all he got for his trouble—yet it remained a wound greater than all others had managed. Sturmund saw with greedy eyes, but before he could test Ghost's discovery, the beast flexed its back legs, coiling down on itself, before exploding upwards, escaping the tumult of their arms, abandoning the field of battle for a stage of baleful shadows.

"Fight, you coward," roared their Captain, swiveling to face the shimmering shadows, each time finding only empty, mocking darkness.

The feral shape darted—swift approaches, sudden feints, wild strafes—never once close enough to reach with sword tip, always hugging the shadows, a white blur in the nasty dark. The galloping terror caused the ground to quake with its blistering speed, but Sturmund and his men were undeterred. They had learned much of the creature's deceitful ways, and like the best warriors, would not be taken in a second time. Tricks and cunning—a beast would not flee if a beast could not be killed. That was the one thing Sturmund knew for certain.

"Form tight," Sturmund called, and together the five closed ranks.

They moved more surely than before, steady strides into the dark, towards the thrashing shadows and trembling ground. There would be no more waiting. The warriors did not possess the years as did the beast. Their lives were short—too short to wallow in fear. They would bring the fight on their own terms.

The beast did not approve. A sudden dash from cover, the beast lurching out from thick brush, jaws reaching for Patch, who still struggled with Marney's blood staining his vision red. Like all things that hunt, the beast had a sense for the weak, but Culp and Bitch rose to strengthen their struggling comrade, lending their arms to drive the creature back to the darkness, where it went, throwing long, resentful wails.

Again and again, the battle dragged—violent sorties by the sly beast, stalwart counterattacks by the hardy crew. Nothing was taken from the beast, its deft lunges and agile retreats offering no weakness, its tender neck, once touched, always protected.

"This is madness," Patch shouted, his comrades grouped around him in their protective formation. "We can't keep up with it. We need to run."

As if drawn by Patch's doubt, the beast emerged once more from the shadows, bounding towards the exhausted bowman. Dagger followed arrow, neither deterring the charging beast, but the strength of four other arms added to his own, a shining wall of steel and grit assembling on their man, brought Patch through the onslaught unscathed but exhausted.

The skirmish had gone on for long minutes, every foray by the beast claiming more and more of the group's resolve, more and more of their endurance. The attacks had become increasingly severe as the moments dragged on, the beast no doubt sensing the fading vigor of the warrior band. Crash following crash, bone and hide meeting armor and blade—

they fought without cumbersome shields to slow them, Sturmund having taught them to rely upon practiced guards to repel an enemy's assault, a once-winning strategy now sorely tested by the heaving mass of flesh and fury. It remained to be seen how long the group could withstand the siege.

"Courage," was all Sturmund said, an order and a plea, their survival joined, their strength a collective that would not survive a weakening link.

Patch gulped air, trying to quench the burning in his lungs. The darkness around them remained as thick as ever, their position lost in a black sea, castaway figures on an ocean of shadow, no land in sight.

"Stay if you like," Patch said quietly, ruefully, his cheeks flushed. "Die if you like."

As dead a shot as he was, Patch had the bad habit of looking at the world through the wrong eye, so that all he saw was darkness looming, the possibility of a brighter world never occurring to him. None of the other warriors had heard his treasonous sentiments—yet they had not been the only audience that night.

A sickly mewling slunk from the shadows, responding to Patch's doubt. The noise began slowly, winding its leisurely way from the depths of a most vulgar growl up to the treacherous heights of the hacking, frenzied screech that now threatened to stop the blood in the warriors' veins. None of them, in all their violent years, had ever known as chilling a sound—they who were so well acquainted with the meaty lop of flesh, the throaty gurgle of blood-drowned breaths. But who had ever heard a creature laugh in such a way, devoid of mirth and mercy, brimming only with madness.

How were the warriors to know that the wild cackle that rent that evening black was decidedly of the earth, and held a greater claim to it than any tongue of man, for that savage din hailed from an earth long-since vanished, from before the skies first broke blue or the tides ever thought to set their course. It was a sound from the new-born earth, the vanished earth, a time before language, when the only voice had been the beast's, sovereign and absolute.

Patch swallowed hard, his mouth dry, his throat sore. He could not, however, swallow down his doubts. Those he had loosed into the night, into the darkness, where the beast lived and ruled. Patch's fear now belonged to it.

The beast burst from the shadows, the hail of its cackling a relentless, mocking wind sent to buffet the ears of Sturmund's men. It ran and it did not stop, cutting a sharp line for the group's weak man, the galloping beast mirrored in the single eye so full of regret.

"Together," Sturmund called, and the warriors grouped tightly, bracing for the coming crash, steel thrown up like lattice-work.

All Patch saw was death, and he was not ready.

Mere moments later, when he regained consciousness, Patch woke to a different world. The group had broken, tossed to the winds by the lashing of the beast. Ghost was already on his feet, more than could be said for the rest, and was running, headlong, desperation etched on his pale face, the calm once so familiar to him now nothing but a memory.

Patch struggled to move. He was alive and whole, but battered brutally. His hands shot instinctively to his gut where the deep black of bruising was already blossoming beneath his tunic. He looked from Ghost's pained face and traced the line of the frantic eyes. When Patch saw what had so upset the imperturbable tracker, his heart sank as well.

36

Bitch was alone. Her brothers were all around her—some still waking from the dark, others scrabbling onto unsteady legs, even then rushing to her aid—but Bitch knew she was alone.

Her mind balked at the enormity of the creature—not just its form, but its looming presence, the certainty of death that rose like steam from its sweaty hide.

She could have run, could have fled, perhaps to steal another day from fate. But her mind, even then, faced with the impossible wrath of the frenzied beast, could think of no worse hell than a day in which she lived poorly where others died well.

She did not run; she did not flee. She remained, and, in that stony defiance, she recalled—not for the first time that day, nor the thousandth time since joining with her Captain—the compact to which she had gladly signed away her life, and the man to whom she had given over her soul.

Nor did she lay down her arms, useless as she knew they were. Through her nose, she drew cold breath, like chilled fire it brought life into her beating breast. The ground shook, but her balance kept. The words of their oath rang in her mind, the man who had spoken them to her never far from her thoughts.

She lowered her curved sword, down from the high, heavy guard, now to a reckless, defiant pose, both hands bracing the hilt against her scarred stomach, the wicked blade now a taunting, warding spike.

The beast felt her defiance like a slap against its sweaty hide, and with a low growl, drove on.

If the beast wished to have her for its supper, Bitch would make sure it was a meal on which it would choke. Let it but fall on her blade as herself, and she would think the trade fair. This alone, she prayed.

The thunder stopped, the eye of the storm and its false calm surrounding her. The beast had come.

Bitch glared. The hulking creature loomed and reared— forepaws raised, poised, and then falling.

Bitch never blinked, even as the beast came down, a crashing tower, stone-like hooves lashing, great slabs of muscle opposing, and she, so small, lost within its shadow —the gnashing teeth and lecherous grin, the sickly hide blanched by time, slick earth smeared like war paint, patches of festering moss growing like a pox. Worst of all, the eyes—dead things, no light or life within the twin voids. And with no spark of the creature's own to fill their vacant dark, Bitch found her own self lost in their abyss, every moment of her life shining in those blind-black spheres— the terror and pain of her youth, the terror and the pain of her adulthood—all reflected back in the dull waters of loveless eyes.

This, then, was an ending, and it had been coming all along. So when she and her death had been as near as pages of a closed book, Bitch could not for the life of her understand how between herself and the beast had come her Captain.

Steel flashed as did teeth, Sturmund grinning as he laid his blade into the lurching neck, proving to himself once more that sharp steel and proud hearts can bring any beast to task.

The hide was monstrously thick, tougher even than the warrior's plate, but the blade was sharp and oiled, always readied, as was its master. The blade cut, and the creature bellowed, wild and insane.

To every corner of the stretching forest the cry of the beast came, rolling like the familiar thunder of its hooves, the savage fear and mad wrath unlike anything the woods had ever known. Birds as far as the horizon departed from their lofty treetop aeries in mad flurries of flapping wing and ruffled feather, their dark shapes taking to frantic skies, clambering always higher, desperate for the thin air and black quiet of evening stillness; while along the ground surged the torrent of claws and tails, furred figures and panicked eyes abandoning den and burrow, warren and lair, the exodus unfolding as the great battle raged.

The beast turned in its charge, a breakneck feint, the sheer force of air thrown by its shifting form knocking Bitch to the ground. The beast had been turned away, but shock at the insult more than fear of the injury had informed its flight. The blade had cut, but it had not cut deep.

Shining steel had pushed through inch after inch of living leather, inch after inch of raw muscle. And then it had stopped, all Sturmund's power unable to drive it further. It had stopped, and it had broken—Sturmund's steel and Sturmund's smile both.

Bitch watched, horrified, as the events unfolded—her death stolen with her Captain.

The events unfolded with cruel swiftness. Sturmund fell beneath the beast—dragged effortlessly under foot as the creature fled, drawn an impossible distance over rock and through tree, along savage earth and under savage beast.

"Let go!" Bitch was surprised to hear herself scream out—some part of her mind still able to form thought.

Sturmund had not heard her. He was in the thunder, perhaps dead already, though his body, like his spirit, remained undeterred. Thick, powerful hands gripped the vicious hide from below, fingers relentless, arms burning. The ground flashed by, taking bits of him away with it as it scathed and scraped. The pain was unyielding; the pain was nothing.

Sturmund grinned and sunk his fingers deeper into the hateful skin, the beast groaning at the wrenching of its flesh. Sturmund held fast, the capsized Captain riding the godly beast, racing the lonely path, knowing a day had come. He did not let go.

As long as he could breathe...

37

The beast went screaming through the forest, insane with rage at the impertinence of mortal hands. It had cast off the impudent tick, trampled it well beneath its feet, grinding feeble bones with twisting hooves, mashing the flesh to the pulp it was. It was not meant for such low creatures to draw a god's blood, yet now twice in as many moonrises the sacrilege, the desecration, the profanity.

The beast stomped the ground in petulant wrath, ripping the earth with its murderous hooves. Black clouds of heaving dirt billowed into the breezy air. Smoke without fire hovered above the treetops; a growing storm cloud without any rain.

For millennia the beast had lorded over its forest realm —since before the time of men, and now since the time of men. Yet for all its countless years, the beast was but a child compared to the ancient things with which it shared the world—ageless beings that dwelt within the silent ground and under the sunless seas, inside the lonely mountains and circling the dark skies above.

But the beast knew nothing of such primal existences and so believed itself alone, a ruler of a dying world, a king without a cause. In the ceaseless loneliness of years unending, the beast succumbed to madness, and in that madness, believed itself a god.

38

They found him an hour's journey from where he had been taken. Ghost followed the tracks, head down, crestfallen, but the trail of blood and ruin was clear for all who had eyes to see. In a clearing of fallen trees, trunks smashed and splintered, they found him.

"We need to take him back." They all looked at her, knowing she was right, none sure of how it could be done.

What little remained of the body had been crushed almost beyond recognition—bones snapped, limbs pulverized, a gruesome sight even for a band who had believed themselves beyond shock of violence.

"We should come back for him," Culp said, the depth of his voice scraping the bowels of the Earth. "We leave him for now."

Had anyone else said the words, Bitch might have struck him, but she knew Culp as a man of honor, and heard him out, even if her mind was already set.

"We follow the path," Culp said, pointing with his sword blade down the rut of earth carved by the beast's flight. "It's on the run. Sturmund was right. It's a coward. We should finish it now while it still fears us. It's what the Captain would do."

"Fears us?" Patch laughed. "It ate Marney in one bite. Just fucking ate him like he were nothing more than a dormouse. Look at the Captain," he said, pointing insolently at the smear of remains. "And you think this thing's afraid of *us*?"

Culp drew back his upper lip, his contempt for Patch as bared as his teeth. "I wasn't speaking to you. I was speaking to the warriors who remain. Go back home, little boy."

Patch kept his smile, nor had he altered a single muscle on his face, yet somehow his looks took on a viciousness almost palpable.

"You think you could take me on, oaf? Could you reach me before my arrows take you? I've killed twice as many men as you."

"Twice as many women and children, perhaps," Culp said, spitting the words. "You are the better killer, but you are no warrior." Culp then looked away, a slight more severe than any word or slap, for it said to the other how little threat he posed.

With reflexes decades in the making, Patch reached over one shoulder, his bow never more than a moment's grasp away. Ghost struck him hard in the kidney, then again in the tender spot below his chest when the one-eyed killer turned to retaliate.

"That's enough," said Bitch. She had placed herself between the men, preventing Culp from dropping his blade between Patch's good eye and his patch. "We bring Sturmund home, we regroup and tend to our wounds. Agreed?"

Ghost nodded. Culp looked again to the wreckage of trees and to the wreckage of his Captain. For once, he allowed his wisdom to lead his temper. He nodded.

"Good," Bitch continued, rattling off orders with calm disdain, a born leader. "You're not needed, Patch. You can go. Sturmund isn't here to cast judgment on you. There's no more oath to break. It died with our Captain."

"Very tough you all are," Patch said between labored breaths. He had fallen to one knee, catching his wind and biding his time. "With just enough brains to get yourselves killed."

"Shut up, Patch." Bitch was a moment away from letting Culp off his leash.

"That's what you all want, isn't it? Chasing a monster, and not the other way around." Patch encompassed them all in the bitter derisiveness of his laugh. "You sick bastards, you all *want* to die. Just like him. There's no glory in death," he said, finally standing. "There's only this shit—bloody skid marks and a mangled corpse. It's fucking pathe—"

Bitch was on him. Patch had been ready for it, for one of them to make their move. He knew how best to goad them. Still, the ferocity of her assault surprised even him. They hit the ground hard, Bitch pinning him with her legs as she raged.

"You weak little shit," Bitch yelled in his face. She brought her fist down with each word. "After everything Sturmund did for you."

It was as far as she got. Patch had let her get close, glad for once to have felt the heat of her body atop his, and when he tired of her, he cast her aside, like all the others. She hit the tree behind him after Patch drove his knee into her stomach and carried the momentum backwards, flipping her head over heels.

Ghost and Culp approached, weapons drawn, but Patch had rolled away in the same movement that had sent Bitch sailing, only to rise with daggers outstretched and all three fighters to his front. Warrior or not, Patch was as savvy a killer as any of them knew, and none was eager to test their luck.

Ghost remained silent, and deadly in his calm. Culp, too, had no words, only seething anger as he gripped his sword hilt, his eyes counting the steps and Patch's likely countermoves.

It was Bitch who broke the stalemate; Bitch, who of them all, had reason most to wish Patch ill.

"How can you care so little? Did he really mean nothing to you?"

She had risen from the ground, brushing off the dirt, pretending that her ribs were not cracked. She spoke in a vacant way, not unkindly, but with nothing that suggested she was speaking to anything human. She kept her arms at her sides, but Patch knew, as did the rest of them, that Bitch was most deadly when underestimated.

"I never said that," Patch said, his eye staring directly at Ghost as he spoke. The pale figure stood between Bitch and Culp, allowing Patch's limited periphery to encompass all three fighters.

"You would have been dead years ago if he hadn't taken you in."

"You think I don't know that?" Patch's voice broke as he snapped, his words echoing in the silent glade.

A little boy hated by his mother. The child of rape, cursed from birth—by birth—cast out when barely old enough to fend for himself. A little boy unloved by all, one hug from a mother all he wanted, the hand that lashed him back taking his eye and his heart in the single swipe. That was who spoke with Patch's lips in the cold of the forest, the little boy against the world, suspicious of everyone, covetous of everything.

"Then be the man he saw in you." Something in Patch's voice had shaken her from her purpose, and she kept the dagger where it lay, hidden up her sleeve.

"It's what he would have wanted," Patch said, looking past Ghost to where Sturmund lay. "It's all he ever wanted."

"I know," Bitch said, unsure if Patch was referring to Sturmund's death or something else entirely.

"We can use my new cloak to wrap him." Patch lowered his knives and drew the gray wool from his satchel. He held it in his hands, coddling it foolishly, uncertainly. "I took it off Marney's pack."

Ghost lowered his sword. Culp did not.

"Then that is what we will do," Bitch said, and she walked over to Patch and took the cloak.

When she turned her back to him, it did not slight him. It honored him.

BLIND EYE

"That's the one I mean, Captain. Over by the whores."

"Who? Him? You can't be serious. He's got one bleedin' eye fer fuck's sake."

"Pipe down, you red bastard. I was speaking to the Cap'n."

"I'll speak whenever I damn well please you raspy sack of bones."

"Raspy? Why you blubbery bastard. I'd like to see you take a thrust to the throat. See how pretty you sing after."

"Blubbery? This is all muscle. Listen. You hear that. That's the sound of steel."

"I don't hear shit. But your stomach is still jiggling."

"It's a protective layer."

"Enough, both of you."

"Aye, Captain."

"Aye, sir . . . but it *is* all muscle underneath. I want it known."

"Quiet, you boob. Here he comes—Now, watch his hands, Captain."

"Excuse me, gentlemen. Let me just . . . pardon me. My

you're a big fellow. Just need to squeeze past here. Many thanks."

"Did you see that, Captain?"

"I did."

"See what? Why are you laughing?"

"'My you're a big fellow.' What balls."

"Tell me."

"How much coin do you have on you, Hull?"

"None of your damn business, you old goat."

"Just show me."

"Alright, but I'm not buying you any more ale until you tell me what's so funny. Here, I've got . . . what? Where the hell is my bloody purse. You old thief, what have you done with it? I'll wring your—"

"Calm, Hull."

"But Captain, Marney's stolen my coin."

"It was not our Scholar. Take a look at the young man paying his tab. Such a fine leather purse he draws his coin from, no?"

"I'll crush his skull."

"No, Hull!"

"Get off of me, Marney."

"A little help, Captain?"

"Why won't you let me kill him. Alright, alright, I'm calm."

"Quiet. He's looking. Don't let him see anything is amiss. Alright, he's not noticed—Captain, he's got quick hands. We could use such a man."

"Only a fool invites a thief into his fold."

"Ah, but Captain, cunning and stealth are so easily undervalued. Replace the empty hand with the silent blade, and how readily the cut-purse becomes the cut-throat. Very useful, indeed."

"Perhaps."

"Ach, you're crazy, Marney. We don't need scrawny sneaks. Our company needs warriors, needs men. Like the one Sinner was speaking of the other day. That potter he saw cleave the man in two at the market. Now there's a worthy recruit."

"Sinner is a madman and can't be trusted worth a damn."

"Sinner is the best damn killer I've ever laid eyes on—No offense meant to yourself, Captain. You fight like the lion—And you know damn well, Marney, 'twas the witch's poison did fer his and Bob's minds. I still trust his sense a damn sight more than yours. If Sinner says the potter's our man, then we should be wasting no more time here on your dainty little pickpocket."

"You have a mouth that says everything and eyes that see nothing."

"I have a hammer that says all I need. No tricks, only iron. And at least I have both my eyes unlike your cyclops over there."

"I am inclined to agree with Hull, Scholar. I would trade a dozen assassins for one stalwart blade."

"Here, here, Captain. A company of men. Not that our old sawbones would know anything about it."

"Mind yourself, Hull. Our Scholar has forgotten more of tactic and maneuver than either of us may ever know."

"I thank you for the words, but I take no offense from a mouth that is so often catching flies. Now, Captain, if you would permit—an experiment?"

"As you wish."

"Hull, you have been wronged. I see that I was misguided. It must be my years catching up with me. Go collect your coin and your apology."

"Now you speak sense, you old goat. Ha, ha!—Boy! Yes, you there. You have something of mine, and I have something fer you."

"Twenty pieces on our one-eyed friend."

"I know you would never bet against one of our own, Scholar."

"Of course not, Captain. I merely jest. I am sure Hull will prevail . . . so long as he keeps his head."

"RAHH!"

"And right through the table—Get up, Hull—I'm sure it was just a lucky feint, Captain."

"Damn, rabbit! Stay still and fight like a—BAH!"

"And there goes the door. Shall we finish the drink or go join them outside, Captain?"

"Let us go, Scholar. I should like to see how the boy handles himself when Hull gets angry."

"Oh! They're back inside. I must say, Captain, even flying through the window, the boy cuts a rather graceful figure."

"Ha! Now, that's how you throw a body, lad. No, no, you just lie right there. Just let me give you this before you—"

"Do not boast, Hull. Stay on your guard. Watch the leg."

"—gods almighty!"

"Too late, Captain—What are you crying about, Hull? You never wanted to sire children anyway. Shake it off."

"No, Scholar. Our warrior has been bested. Let us collect him, quickly."

"Yes, sir—Here now, boy, just leave off. That's right stop your wailing on him. That face of his can't stand getting any uglier. Hey, now—"

"Scholar, the dagger!"

"—you tricky little shit!"

"Leave the blade in, Scholar. It will help staunch the flow—Calm yourself, boy. My name is Stur—"

"Cap'n, another one! Where is he pulling all these blades from? Here, Captain, behind the table with me!"

"I do not hide."

"Get down! Gods almighty. Nearly shaved your mane, sir. I counted six, ah, plus this shiny new splinter in my arm. Are you hit, sir?"

"Yes."

"Is it bad? Let me see."

"He fights like a thing possessed."

"He must be out of steel. And this table won't shelter us forever. Do we chance a charge?"

"He hasn't run. He is either very foolish, or very dangerous."

"I think I can guess which. What's he doing now? Let me look—Well, he's not out of blades. Damn near opened my melon—He's just sitting there on Hull's gut, smiling. Something's wrong with this one. I regret getting us into this mess."

"Regret nothing, Scholar. When this day is done, we will have either breathed our last or learned a valuable lesson. I am content with either path."

"Yohoo! Hey, you there. Old man. Blondie. What are you two waiting for? Everyone else has cleared out. Now's your chance. I promise I won't stab you repeatedly as you flee—just the once."

"Your generosity would shame a king. Let us return the sentiment by giving you the opportunity to surrender, my boy. We'll hang you nice and quick. What do you say? Have you come to your senses yet?—Captain, let's do a pincer."

"Hey, are you two thinking about a pincer move? That's probably what I would do . . . if I were a couple of idiots."

"You fight with heart, but you are arrogant and reckless. Do not presume yourself victor until the blood has cooled."

"Wise words, Captain, but what, exactly, is our plan?"

"We do what we have always done when death calls on us to raise our necks: we present them."

"Oh, Captain, I'm not so sure—"

"I hope you two aren't thinking about making any sudden movements. I would hate to have to slice this oaf's throat. These are new trousers I have on. Just throw down your arms and hand over your purses, or he dies. Then, maybe I'll consider sparing you."

"We will save our man if we can, but make no mistake, if his life—my life, our lives—are the price of your defeat, I will pay it."

"That's quite . . . the team spirit. Very inspiring."

"Oh, Captain, there's that glint in your eye. I really suggest we—"

"Now, Scholar!"

"Yes, sir."

"You crazy sons of—Get off of me! Ech, you're bleeding in my mouth. Pah!"

"Now, if I were you, boy, I would stay very, very still."

"Scholar, do you have rope?"

"You wound me more deeply than this blade in my shoulder—or this one in my leg, or, oh look, this one in my other shoulder that I just noticed. Of course I have rope, sir. I have everything."

"Get it. I will hold our man."

"I am not your man. And I don't know what you two think you're going to do with me tied up, but know this—on no account will I let you deflower me. I am as chaste as a spring day."

"And I am the king of these here kingdoms, eh, Captain? Here's the rope. I'll do the hands, if you'll manage the legs, sir."

"I'll cut you for this. In all the tender places. Slow and sure, I'll make you bleed."

"Shall we gag him, Captain? Ah, but we're low on rope. Guess we'll just have to cut the tongue off."

"You'll do no such thing, you old cocksucker."

"Gods almighty, but you have a vile mouth on you, boy—I was only joking about the tongue, sir, but maybe we reconsider?"

"Not yet. But if he spits any more fire, feel free—Now, young fighter, I would speak with you. Whether you listen is your choice. Know this, much depends on your hearing the words of the warrior."

"I await with bated breath."

"I am Sturmund, Captain of a company of the finest blades in the kingdom. We number twenty, at present. More each day join our ranks. We fight for—"

"Twenty? My gods, look how proud you are saying that. Twenty? And you're telling me you haven't already taken the King's Keep with all your horde?"

"You're a fine and fearsome blade. Untied and on your feet, how many men could you kill before you fell to overwhelming odds?"

"As many as came on."

"And if there were twenty of you. How many then?"

"But there you are mistaken, O, mighty warrior-king. There is only one Patch in all the lands. Not a one of your rabble could even hold a candle to me. And so, much as I may wish otherwise, I shall always be alone."

"Pardon my interrupting, sir. But I feel obliged to point out to our young captive here that lovely bit of irony, he being in his position, we being in ours. Wizened and infirm as we are, eh? Couldn't even manage the three of us, the poor lamb."

"Well, I'm not the old fool who tied his captive's hands behind his back, now am I?"

"How's tha—Captain, he's loose!"

"Not this time, young fighter."

"Good shot, Captain—Nice try, boy. Fair enough. We'll just keep those hands where we can see them from now on. How did you do that, anyway? I learned that knot from Strange Bob, and when he's not shitting or killing, he's talking about knots."

"As if I'd tell you. And what the fuck is a Strange Bob?"

"Keep it up, boy, and I'll introduce you. I promise, you will rue the meeting."

"Enough, Scholar—Young fighter, this is your final chance. Heed the words of the warrior, or face your end."

"Gods, does he talk like that all the time? It's really too much. If I had to listen to that all day, I don't know what—"

"Cut his throat, Scholar."

"With pleasure, Captain."

"Whoa, whoa, easy grandfather. Put down the knife."

"Orders is orders, boy. Ain't my call. Now, let's see, right-to-left? That's gypsy style. Or left-to-right? That's, of course, the way the priests do it. Are you a god-fearing boy? Of course you are. That settles it, then. And here. We. Go."

"Alright, I'm listening. I hear you. I don't want to die. Call him off."

"There is no shame in dying, young fighter. That is not the lesson."

"Well what is? Huh? What do you want from me? To fight with you? Fine, sign me up. Count me in. Whatever it takes to get you old maniacs off of me."

"You still are not hearing."

"I heard every fucking thing you said. Thirty men. Finest blades. Join the cause."

"No, young fighter. You have not listened carefully. You have been listening to me. I have told you to hear the words of the warrior, he who resides within you, within us all."

"Oh, gods, I've changed my mind. Cut my throat already."

"Don't tempt me, boy."

"You told me you are alone and always shall be."

"I'm just that good."

"No, but you could be. In time. With training. A true warrior."

"I've gotten by this far without the likes of you."

"You will die badly without us."

"And you'll save me? Keep me safe and strong?"

"No, you will die badly without us. You will die well in our company. I can save you only from shame. What else is there of consequence?"

"Pussy. Gold. Meat. Drink. Smoke. Ease and comfort. Power and control."

"Emptiness."

"Yeah, well it suits me fine."

"Who are your people?"

"I told you, I am alone. Always have been. Always will be. Now fuck off. You don't even have to untie me, just fuck right off out of here."

"No one is born alone, young fighter. Your father, what was his profession?"

"Rapist."

"Something tells me the apple didn't exactly fall—"

"Silence, Scholar!"

"Sir."

"Oh, you really know how to keep 'em in line, eh, Sturmy?"

"We are not always destined to follow in the paths of our

forebears. Believe me, young fighter. I more than most, perhaps, can speak to that."

"Daddy was mean to you?"

"Not once did my father ever treat with me without honor. Nevertheless are we dead to each other."

"He's dead?"

"He lives, but not as my father."

"I'd be awfully curious to know what kind of man it takes to raise a child like you."

"You may already."

"What the hell does that mean? You trying to say you're my father? Because if so, I'd be curious to know who the last father I gutted was."

"No, young fighter. I am not your father, nor do I know who the man is. I was merely speaking of my own father. If you come to our company, perhaps one day I would tell you of him."

"Tempting as that is—"

"And what of your mother, does she live still?"

"You shut your fucking mouth about my mother!"

"Good, there is passion in you, and not merely rot. Your past is your affair. We will speak no more of it."

"Let me go."

"Make your choice."

"No."

"You refuse my offer, then."

"I refuse your demand. When I decide where my path leads, it will be on my own terms, and in my own time."

"A worthy sentiment."

"Then you'll release me?"

"No. Nor will I repeat my terms. The offer has been made. It stands, even now. Whether you take it remains, as you say, your choice. And you may take it in your own time, such few minutes as remain to you."

"Well, say something, boy. Answer the Captain."

"I'm thinking."

"Think faster."

"Everyone I have ever known has abandoned me, turned on me. If I join you—"

"Eh? Er. Bawrrmhh."

"Uh-oh. Hull's coming back to us, sir."

"Send him back to the dark. Now is no time for distraction."

"Understood."

"Who's that? Marney? Give a hand and help me—"

"Night, night, you big oaf."

"Wait just a blasted mo—"

"He's out."

"What was it you asked, young fighter?"

"Nothing. It doesn't matter—Hey, old man, what do you say to my joining your company of fools?"

"The Scholar has done his speaking for the day. Is the question important to you?"

"Yes."

"Then I may answer for him, for I know his mind and his heart as well as I do my own. Our Scholar would not wish you to join our company. Once, he had a mind to recruit you. What he has seen of you today has challenged his faith in the prospect. Now, he would rather you refuse so he might slit your throat and be done with you. He is not so wrong in this. His mind is brilliant, and his logic is not in error. You are foolhardy and inexperienced, and the cruelty in you blinds you to all else.

"Ours is not a company of fools. Nor of killers. We walk the path of warriors. The road is difficult, and it will not

We Burn Our Dead

suffer the weak—the weak of mind, the weak of body, and, most of all, the weak of heart. You are deficient in all three, and there is not a one among the thirty men who would see it differently. Thirty men stand against you, then. Fortunately for you, theirs is not the voice that matters.

"I offer you this chance, and therefore do thirty others, who will accept you wholly as their brother for life. It is not your past that interests me, nor the pain you carry. What I see in you is fire—brilliant, perhaps blinding. And that is also where the danger lies. Fire can temper, strengthen. More often, fire melts, destroys. Which fire is yours remains to be seen. But the path of the warrior is not one of safety, and so with this offer, know that I wager not your life only. Now, make your choice."

"I . . . I accept your offer."

"Why?"

"Because it is my choice."

"Then I welcome you to the ranks of the last profession you will ever know. You will die in this company. But fear not—you will be born here as well."

39

Those who remained built the fire together. Bitch and Patch laid the heavy timber, white elm and sacred ash tree that Culp and Ghost had brought back from the woods. Ghost dragged and braced the branches as Culp trimmed and readied them for the pyre. They worked in silence, the occasional grunt of focused labor spurring the others to the task more fiercely still. It was tiring work, but necessary. Their Captain deserved no less.

Patch rose from where he had been laying the kindling in neat bundles along the base of the stack and stretched his back where a knot had begun to ache. Bitch thrust another bundle into his arms, her quiet way of telling him to press on. Patch took the sticks and bent wordlessly to the task.

They had none of them discussed the idea of naming a new Captain for the same reason they had not considered the issue privately. The idea had simply not occurred to them. Each knew that there was to be no more band of men after that night's work was finished. There was no need for a leader amongst strangers and wanderers who set out on separate paths. The time of the warrior had left them behind, stragglers along angry roads, travelers in blood. They were finished. Sturmund was dead, his tired cause with him.

There was a flash of white sparks in the cold air, then darkness as they burnt out. Culp struck the flint again, harder this time, and another flurry of light burst forth, settling to nothing soon after. Ghost approached on silent feet and softly took the stones from Culp. The large man looked at the pale figure with hard eyes, distrustful instincts already growing between them, set like roots at the moment of Sturmund's death, deepening ever since. Ghost did not back down, his eyes glowing with light from a moon paler even than he, and Culp handed him the flint.

In two deft swipes, Ghost had the torch lit. The sparks settled over the dry bundle and brought to roaring life a lifeless thing.

The four stood in the glow of torchlight, in their cloaks looking nothing so much like pagan priests, but their ritual was older than anything such mystics could claim. Their task was the rite of the warrior, the sending off to final rest a man of courage and might.

The torch sputtered in the wind, the tongues of flame lashing out spitefully. For a moment, no one moved. The four seemed transfixed by the small fire, each staring into the fierce blue heart of flame. It was to be the last time they would gather together around a fire, each knowing he bade farewell to more than their Captain that night.

Bitch grabbed the torch from Ghost's hand. He surrendered it willingly. She had again, as ever, proved herself strongest.

The torch took to the air, trailing sparks and fire as it

sailed to the top of the heap where Sturmund rested. For a while there was nothing, the light lost in those high reaches. Then, slowly, came the glowing and the heat. The four watched, together and apart, taking their places, each at one side of the pyre, out of sight from the others yet knowing they were not alone.

The fire grew. Soft, subtle, delicate—a liquid flame pooling along the uppermost portions before snaking quickly through the structure, gaining size and force as it fed on wood and flesh. Before any of them had truly realized, the entire mound had taken flame, a tower of heat and snarling fire twisting in the wind, reaching upwards towards the black and the stars. As he had in life, Sturmund burned once more.

Culp and Ghost, Patch and Bitch, the four remaining warriors watched until the last, stepping back only when the scorching heat forced them, their skin red and burning, eyes bleary with heady smoke.

As the flames died and the embers smoldered, after the pyre had collapsed, the walls coming down in a thunderous crash that sent eruptions of churning sparks into the sky, the four were revealed to one another again, each still at his post, faces caked in ash, clothes in soot. Their eyes had kept something of Sturmund's fire, a painful light still glowing within, and in silent, motionless accord, they decided their fate.

Culp turned first; Ghost and Bitch close behind. Only Patch hesitated, but even then, only for a moment. He hastened to catch up to the figures following the inland trail, back into the shadowed forest, towards the lair of the beast, the home of death.

He stopped at the treeline and gave a look back to the

We Burn Our Dead

world, to the open sky and star-flaked night, the fields of grass and well-worn paths, the empty camp and Sturmund's mound. Without a sound, he disappeared, off after those strangers and warriors, his brothers and his sister.

40

The beast lurched up the slope, chasing the morning. Great legs pumping, it threw itself upwards, hugging the rock face as it went, its hulking frame reckless on the narrow climb. The precipitous drop looked down on distant treetops, hazy in the mist of early morning, the sound of roaring waters growing the further it climbed.

The falls lay in the green heart of the sprawling forest, where surging waters rushed down the cliffside before plummeting gracefully, powerfully, from craggy heights and sudden drops. A pristine oasis, sacred to the beast, the summit stood untouched by all other creatures. To its lofty perch the beast returned. On the high ground it would be safe. That is what the beast needed to believe.

It was wounded—not physically, though its bloated belly ached from where a man had wrenched its skin, its neck chafing with the scratch of careless steel, its eye stinging from a stray arrow. It remained strong, as a god must, but was wounded nonetheless. The injury it nursed lay deeper than any sword or bolt could pierce. The wound it felt was fearfulness, and the insult to its pride.

We Burn Our Dead

It was not meant for gods to dread, nor would the beast suffer itself to doubt. To the top of its forest it had fled, and, through centuries of sleep, would soon forget the disheartening hours that had befallen it, wishing nothing so much, as it settled into unshakable slumber, that the sun would soon set on that most strange of days.

41

Life had done little to bring them together. They none of them shared any affection for the world of men, the taste of breath always stale in their mouths. It was not life that linked them, but rather death that united them in common cause. And now, reduced to but four souls, better men having been put to ground, sent on ahead to the dark that waited for them all, the warriors journeyed together one last time, as much for themselves as for each other.

They retraced their steps in stony silence, coldly reflecting on the grim cairns they had left behind in the ancient earth—the mud and muck where Hull had taken his fatal fall, the abandoned cave near which wise Marney stood his last, the crater in which Sturmund had been reduced to little more than fragments of the greatness he had been in life. And as they passed, baleful eyes hardening with each painful landmark, there came a point where the path ended, the trail of the beast cut short.

"It ends here," Ghost said when the deep-set tracks finally vanished and the breathtaking slopes appeared.

"It certainly does," said Bitch, looking out over the same

rising ground, where widening treelines and thick flowing grass, untouched and untrampled by rougher forms, opened onto nascent hill and, beyond that, imperious mountain.

"You can track it, Ghost?" Patch spoke very softly, and, wrapped in the unfamiliar gentleness, the words came more as encouragement than question.

Ghost nodded, and with his sword tip showed them the way. From the haft of his gray blade an invisible line extended, along which the solemn eyes followed. The peak was cloud-covered, wreathed in bright morning mist, not of storm or tempest but the hale and hearty white of mythic airs. The storm, the warriors knew, dwelled within that veil, dormant and waiting.

Culp was not impressed, and with a sniff, pushed past the others, tugging his great blade snug against his back as he set off upon the climb. They had all known steeper roads, their entire lives uphill struggles, but the sight of that hazy summit, above which only empty heaven stretched, brought finally into view the end of all journeys—from such heights, there was but one way down.

HELPING HAND

The morning was all bright haze and bracing cold, a perfectly miserable day for an equally wretched part of the country. The hieing of plow animals rang in the distance, and horse dung lent the air a comforting richness that to farmer and soldier alike recalled home and hearth. The sun had been up for the better part of an hour; the lights of the potter's for the better part of two.

The horsemen drew up alongside the houses opposite and sat watching from their saddles a silent moment, breath steaming from within their cowls. Tradesmen and hurrying washer-women gave the figures a wide berth. Strangers to the village were few, their coming always a harbinger of ill tidings—someone's father fallen in the wars, someone's mistress grown overly chatty, someone's debt now come due. The villagers had enough shit upon their own plates to risk a curious glance at the newcomers; the gods of wrath and petty mischief were powers easily distracted, and none wished to call down such fell attentions upon his own roof. The three horsemen were left to their business.

"That's the one," one of the riders said, gesturing with the stump of one hand to the structure across the way.

The potter's hut was a decidedly humble thing in a village of already unassuming dwellings. The craftsman had not even bothered to stop up the thatch walls with moss and clay, and as a result, pale smoke coiled not only from the simple stone chimney, but puffed from countless smaller gaps and cracks all over, giving the hut something of the air of a boiling pot.

"You want I should go and talk with our friend?" asked another rider, who wore not only a cowl over his mouth but a piece of soiled cloth over one eye.

"You've been with us all of a month," said Stump, "and already you think you can make the approach?"

"I'm just itching to try my hand at it," Patch said. "No offense, Stumpy."

The one-handed man shifted in his saddle, the creak of leather accompanying the shift of his gaze.

"Keep it up, young buck, and I'll take off one of your appendages." Loss of limb had in no way impaired the feral vigor with which Stump fought—tooth and boot filling in for absent fist. "And I do not mean one of your hands."

"Charming. Say, what did they call you before the . . . before you . . . you know." Patch whistled as he nodded to the offending wrist.

"Lopper," Stump said, tugging at his cowl and giving Patch's groin a maniac grin.

"Well," Patch said, unmoved by the threat, "next time be more careful."

"Ah, I see, boy," Stump said, slowly and deadly, gaze lifting as he spoke. "Not your cock, then. Your tongue. That's what you value; that's what I shall take one day."

"Why wait?" The silver spike was already down Patch's

sleeve and in his grip—another word from Stump would find the hungry needle in motion.

But Stump had had done with the boy for the day, and turned his attentions elsewhere.

The spike slipped back to where it dwelt, but the resentment that had called it down in the first place would linger on from that moment until Stump's last.

"I say we move in now. Let me go make the approach." Stump spoke without a hint of tension in his voice or frame, as though the altercation had not occurred. "If he resists, I'll put him down, no harm done."

"If he resists." Patch snorted. "He's three times your size with twice as many hands. Let someone a bit better equipped . . . *hand*le it, eh?" Patch tugged off the cowl and cackled.

"Fucking rat." Stump made ready to drop from his mount. "I'll go and—"

"We do nothing without the Captain." The third rider had finally made his mind known, and both men fell quiet at his words. The voice may have been perfectly calm, perfectly reasonable, but the glint of delirium, the screaming gale and gnashing fire that ran frenzied in the eyes, stopped the conversation cold.

"And lose the advantage?" Patch ventured after a moment, his tongue having shown remarkable restraint in waiting so long to wag. "If we get the drop on this—"

"There is no surprise." The calm voice spoke; the wild eyes flared.

The faint lamplight showing within the potter's hut had dimmed and almost extinguished as a broad figure crossed its path and came closer the front wall and its myriad apertures. The riders were not the only watchers that morning.

A moment later, the shadow shifted, receding deeper into the hut, and the faint light returned.

"When we make our approach," the mad-eyed rider said, "we knock."

"Knocking," Patch said blithely, balling one fist and making a rapping gesture at Stump. "Your skill set is at last required."

"Cunt."

Patch beamed.

"I will ride to the hillside and watch for Sturmund," the mad-eye said. "Remain here, and watch."

"And if he tries to take a powder?" Stump asked, hopefully.

The rider turned his horse and the terrible gaze fell upon both men. "This one will not run."

Patch waited until the sound of their companion's hoofbeats had faded before dismounting and starting for the door.

"Don't be daft," Stump called, entirely unheeded. "If that devil in there doesn't kill you, then the other one surely will when he gets back and finds you disobeyed him."

Patch offered a gesture without looking back. A moment later he was at the door. A moment after that, he was inside. There was no knocking.

"Oh, what's the fucking use." Stump slunk from the horse, grabbed his sword and disappeared around the rear of the hut.

The heat of kilns baked the air within the hut and drove back the biting winds that whistled through the thatch. The cheek that flushed with brisk morning air glowed brighter still in the sparkling heat.

Patch was not surprised to find a man of such proportions. He had set eyes upon larger brutes in his years. What he had not anticipated was seeing such bulk set to this most delicate of occupations.

"So this is the china shop," Patch said, looking around at the walls of vase and urn, jar and pot, all masterfully crafted, all exceedingly overstocked. "I guess that makes you the bull."

The giant did not look up from behind the massive workbench, nor from the shapely vase he tended to. He ran a damp cloth over the dried clay, revealing a rich, earthen luster. Only when the task was finished and the vase positively glowed did he set the pot down carefully, almost tenderly.

The giant stared at Patch, and waited, saying with his eyes as much as his bearing that the next words out of the visitor's mouth had better be about earthenware.

"You killed a man at the Hawker's market. About four weeks ago," Patch added, to avoid confusion with any slaughter that may have come before or since.

The giant looked on, bored.

"Not ringing any bells? Market. Murder. Trader cut in two—and not the easy way, mind you. I mean, cut in two clean down the middle." He made a chopping gesture with a straightened palm. "Crown to balls."

Silence.

"Uh-huh." Patch felt a the prick of sweat begin at his brow. "Turns out, when you go around dissevering upstanding citizens, their families and friends tend to take notice."

A true lather had broken out along Patch's brow. There

was no doubt the lid was going to come off the hut; the question was simply when.

"Here's how it is—the merchant's guild has put a contract out on you, and we—"

The zweihander was up and in the air faster than Patch would have believed possible. An instant later, it was through the workbench, collapsing the stolid oak table as though it were nothing more than matchstick. Nothing now stood between Patch and the giant, and all advantage fled the one-eyed killer in the cramped confines of the hut.

"Hold it, hold it!" But the blade would not be reasoned with, for it was with the blade that Patch now treated, the giant wielding the steel just the mindless engine that drove the slaughter headlong.

Ceramic shards tore up the dusty air as blade and body collided with their delicate shells. A miasma of clay powder choked and blinded. It was with no small relief to Patch, just then tripping on an overturned rack of pots and crowded by the looming giant, that Stump had seen fit to join the fracas.

There was a groan of displeasure—a low, sonorous lament that shook the hollow space—as the thin blade slid through the outer wall of the hut and into the leaning shoulder of the brute. The blade retreated, only to reappear a moment later from another point some feet away, but the giant had grown wary and kept his distance from the walls of his home. Patch took the opportunity to scramble out of trampling distance.

"Stump," Patch yelled. "Get. The fuck. In here."

"Did you tell him we don't want to kill him?" came the voice from outside.

"He doesn't care."

The giant came on, having caught his breath and

charging once more. But Patch, too, had rallied, and bounded out of reach of blade and brute.

Stump made his entrance—rather gracefully, Patch thought. The one-handed swordsman somersaulted through the door and lost no time distracting the giant with lunges of narrow blade and swift kicks of steel-toed boot. While this unfolded, Patch inched towards the door.

"Don't you even think about it," Stump said, tumbling in Patch's direction, and in so doing, bringing the giant down on both their heads.

The flurry of forms that followed, the singing steel, the kicking heel, provided Patch's enterprising mind with delightful possibility. As Stump was otherwise engaged, and the giant far too single-minded for any last minute diversions, it fell upon Patch to capitalize on the pleasures of the moment.

It was a simple slide of the foot, a graceful shift of weight, a subtle extension of the toe; and Patch had managed to dance clear the singing steel, all while catching Stump in the man's own maneuver. Stump managed one syllable of surprise as Patch tripped him, before the giant's blade removed the left half of his face and skull.

For a moment, Stump, formerly Lopper, was of two minds—one eye staring up from the dusty ground, the other looking out at Patch from atop the dumb legs and wobbling torso. Then the two halves came to an agreement, and the remainder of the already-dead flesh collapsed in a heap.

As much as he may have wished to revel in his cunning deceit, the time was far too rife with chance of misstep. The heavy blade kept falling, carried on as easily as though it were a feather, but with consequence far too devastating to be denied. What daggers hit their mark, landed only with dull thud into duller body. The drama neared its final act.

Patch did not need both eyes to tell him death had caught him out at last. The giant's blade hummed as it sliced nearer. Patch's breath came ragged as his options became far fewer.

The next would be the fatal blow; neither man could have doubted it. The giant did not smile as he raised the hilt, as Patch most certainly would have done. Somehow the absence of any taunt or jest seemed cruel to Patch in his final moment.

The indifferent steel arced its course, its momentum never faltering. At the same time, the side of the hut burst into splinters, the man emerging through the thatch never hesitating. And the two implacable powers met at the apex of their assaults.

Patch could have shat. As it was, he just got the fuck out of the way, grateful and disbelieving in equal measure.

His companion had diverted the blade, had simply strolled through the wall and reached out with the flat of his hand. Who had ever seen such a thing? Who could have ever thought it up?

But there Patch stood, incredulous witness to the mayhem as it even then unfolded.

To his credit, the giant had not dwelt on the unexpected arrival, nor did he offer any generosity to a man who fought without a blade. Empty hands and cold steel clashed.

As was always the way when overwhelming force met with merely impressive skill, the bout did not last long. Two or three deft movements; an equal number of relentless blows; and the giant was on his knee, then knees, then stomach.

"Gods be damned," Patch said, eyeing his companion in the new light, which quite literally shone through the madman-sized whole in the hut.

Wild eyes turned Patch's way, and he regretted calling down their attention.

"You were told to wait." The voice was not angry. Only a sane man rages, where the mad mind merely accepts. "Now we have lost a brother." The figure prodded Stump with an inquisitive toe. "It remains to be seen if we shall replenish the loss."

"My coin'd be on no." Patch eyed the giant heap of muscle and groans that was beginning to stir.

Just then, a shadow flit across the room as another figure stepped through the hole in the wall.

"Captain," both men said.

The fallen giant seemed to rouse at the sight of new arrival, drawn to its presence.

"I am Sturmund," the dour figure said, looking down with stony resolve. "The young warrior is Patch." No one stopped the giant as he raised himself to his knees, even from that position able to meet Patch at an even stare. "You have met Sinner, I believe."

The wild-eyed warrior offered a surprisingly formal nod to his defeated opponent. The giant did not return the compliment.

"Stump," the Captain said, glancing down at his fallen man, "had been of our number since before he was called such. A spirited warrior, you no doubt discovered."

The giant did not answer. His breathing had slowed as he readied himself for reprisal. Violence seldom takes but a single life.

"Our course," Sturmund said, sensing the tension, "depends entirely upon your decision. There is no debt of honor between brothers." So saying, Sturmund crossed his scarred hands in front of himself. "I await your answer."

The giant's eyes narrowed, his brief sojourn into the

dark leaving him with shadows in his mind and doubt on his lips. "What answer?"

It was Sturmund's turn to doubt. The blue eyes narrowed ominously. "You didn't tell him?"

The question was directed to Patch alone, and he was grateful the eyes had not accompanied it.

"Well, you see, Captain—" the rogue began.

Sturmund needed to hear no more. "I lead these men. We are a warrior clan, whose mission—"

"Yes." The single word filled the room.

"Yes?" Sturmund doubted.

"You are inviting me to join you?" He looked to Sturmund, who did not contradict him. "Then, my answer is yes."

"Are you fucking kidding me?" Patch threw up his arms. "That's all it takes?"

"*You*," the giant said, "did not ask."

"Well, I was *getting* to it."

"And *you*," the giant said, rising onto his feet and looming almost larger than the room would permit. "You and I will finish this bout."

Sturmund placed himself between Sinner and the giant. "I would not be so quick to cross steel with our Sinner again."

"He did not bring steel to the fight," the giant said, as though to strengthen his argument.

"Be glad of it," Sturmund answered, not even the whisper of a smile on his face. "I doubt much in this life, but never Sinner. He could kill us all if he so wished."

The giant only glared. The praise smacked of challenge.

Sinner took a step closer to the big man, who, though he did not shrink back, lost some of his fire nevertheless.

"We are brothers now," Sinner said, in the same placid tones, with the same crazed eyes.

Sinner extended the hand that only moments earlier had felled him like a tree. The giant took it and squeezed, getting nothing for all his best effort.

As the party left the hut together, Sturmund called out to Patch. "Go back and collect Stump."

Patch stopped in the road. "But he's . . . he's all . . ." Patch made several awkward gestures with his hands to convey some point Sturmund was indifferent to.

"Hey, big guy," Patch called. The giant turned, face and eyes carved of the same stone. "Come give me a hand with this, eh, brother?"

"My name is Culp, one-eye," the giant said. "And the one inside," he said, nodding towards the hut. "He has a hand. Just for you."

None of the three riders smiled, just turned their horses and departed the village, riding out into the hills and towards the thin line of smoke in the distance.

Patch watched them go.

"Cunts," he said peaceably. He turned and trudged back into the hut.

42

The mist carried swiftly across the wind-swept aerie, the harsh light of day dull and lifeless in the fog. The mighty falls poured from steep cliffs, shimmering waters plunging into icy pools far below. All around, the roar of currents rushed, a soothing cradlesong to drown out the mindless clamor in which life persisted. Lonely was the peak on which slept the beast.

In the deafening air, shapes formed in the mist, on silent feet and with silent purpose.

From unhurried slumber the beast woke, disbelieving with greater measure the world on which it opened its heavy eyes than the dream from which it had been torn. It did not rise, merely flit its blind gaze to the light and sky hanging obdurately above its head. With a long-drawn pull of air, the wet nostrils flared and quivered, studying closely the scent and taste, the very essence of its dominion. The intelligence was dire in its report, maddening in its impossibility—the world remained unchanged. The flavor of the skies, the scent of its breath—all unchanged.

The shadows deepened, taking on form and substance, thickening from nothingness, growing as they came.

With steady furor and awful resolve, the beast unfurled itself, rising darkly, smacking its lips with revulsion. No time had passed. It leered blindly at the haze-covered sphere burning through the clouds. It was the same wretched day.

The swords drew soundlessly, cruel eyes staring from behind a wall of mist.

The beast howled, an uncontrollable wrath foaming at its shuddering mouth, knowing as it did that only one creature could be so foolish, only one creature whose arrogance had arms long enough to reach those impossible heights. It had not seen them, the skillful warriors, who neared their mark with blades raised high. It had not seen them, nor had it needed to. Their stench gave them away long before their climb had ever finished.

Four blades gleamed, each sharp as the next, wielded by masters' hands. With unheard whistle they cut the air—and nothing else.

43

They were losing ground, never falling back, yet driven that way nonetheless. The four dug in, leaning into the thrash of hide and bone and teeth that threw itself at them with insistent savagery. Wherever the snapping jaws sought some piece of flesh to tear and rend, a lattice of unyielding steel repelled.

The beast lashed and lunged, testing, probing, sniffing. Into weakness it would sink its fangs and pick apart the wall of men, but no such weakness did it find, the four warriors moving as one, and all the stronger for it.

A slashing limb danced across the mist, and Patch felt the tireless anger that drove it onward. He caught the claw with his blade, stopping it, but only just, his arm and muscles watery. The blade steadied as Culp added his own steel to the parry, and together the two men fought to cast back the flailing beast.

"I have your sword," Culp said through his strain, and the two locked eyes. "And you have mine." And with twinned effort, the two warriors drove back the beast.

The struggle had left all four exhausted, gasping and

coughing in the wet air. Their fire was fading, and soon would expire, but they were not disheartened. Glowing embers scorch hottest, the dead ash upon them mere disguise. And in the crucible that day, the miracle of flame was made manifest once more—the blaze of battle only strengthening, tempering hearts like steel, joining warriors forever in the flames. If there existed any cracks between them, they existed no longer.

The four warriors raised their arms and braced themselves for whatever came, each now as cunning as Patch, as strong as Culp, as focused as Ghost, as unyielding as Bitch.

The beast leered, disgusted. The mewling rose again, the creature's laughter ringing over the crashing waters. It knew it could not be defeated—so too did the warriors. Such details did not interest them.

Bitch hurled a mocking snarl into the hazy air, a slap to the beast that stung more than their blades ever could, and the laughter faltered, drew down.

Silence and the mist held the air, and before the next savage assault could come, a more powerful din struck up.

"On me," Patch said, then letting a bellow of his own rip from his lungs—a man's shout, a warrior's cry.

The weight of three solid bodies braced against his own, and for a moment, as the thrill of their rough power flowed through him, it felt to Patch as if there were other arms and other legs belonging to himself, extensions of himself. This certain knowledge that he was not alone was something new to him.

The creature growled in the mist, a more vicious laugh rising in its throat. But Patch met the cry unafraid, yelling until his chest ached. He had no choice but to laugh and rave in the face of death, his fate now tied to other fates.

Bitch took up her cry again, adding her voice to Patch's

own, Ghost and Culp doing the same, and soon not even the beast could be heard above the laughter of the warriors, not even the crashing of the falls.

Thunder ripped through the air, the beast bursting into their world and down on their heads. Their shield of arms and grit caught, for a moment, the giant heft of beast, and in that moment, what a sight shone in its blind eyes.

Ghost found the calm that had been stolen from him lying atop the darkened waters. It did not belong to the beast, and was Ghost's then and forever more.

Bitch took back her pride—the choking fear once felt in a shadowed forest, never again to rear its shameful head.

Patch, for once, did not take, but gave—an eyeful of impudent defiance, a message scorched onto sightless spheres.

And Culp—Culp had lost nothing to the beast, nor did he have any charity to give. He merely thought the eye a fine trophy, and so reached out and snatched it.

The beast shrieked in pain, the warriors staggering beneath blast of assailing noise and crushing force. The strength of steel was tested and found wanting, the great wall of arms buckling, bending, breaking, though their mettle never wavered.

It had been the warriors' moment, but like all moments, fine as it was, it had not lasted. Still, it had happened, and that is all that mattered.

With one last charge, the beast decided its fate. The warriors, balancing their heels against the last spot of ground before the fall, did not tremble, no single trace of fear or regret featured anywhere on their haughty brows. The same could not be said for the beast, which, when it came, succeeded only in launching the four warriors off the cliff and into legend.

44

Culp opened his eyes. The sound of steel had awoken him, called him back from the dark place, returned him to the living world for a time. Around him, the bodies floated—his comrades, every one known to him as a brother-in-arms, those with whom he had spilt blood and broken bread.

Patch bobbed face down, beyond Culp's reach. Culp floated, too, but on his back, a small portion of his face breaking the surface so he could breathe and see some of the carnage, the rest of him slumped below the water, limp and dying. Bitch floated on her back as well, but her eyes were closed, and Culp feared they must remain so. The only other sign of life was Ghost crawling onto the shore, where he struggled to stand, fell, and lay still.

The clash of steel continued and recalled Culp to himself. Some ways away, a waterfall crashed, the mist of its wake filling the entire arena with moisture through which the sun refracted ghostly and pale, wisps of vapor swirling like phantoms in the breeze. And far above, a ledge, from which terrible heights warriors had fallen, on which terrible heights a warrior still stood. And the beast was with him.

Culp was too far and too weak to say for sure who the dim figure was who struggled with the creature, raining fearsome blows upon the impenetrable hide. Yet Culp knew it was Sturmund—Sturmund who had died; Sturmund who had fought; Sturmund who lived still.

Culp laughed, a hearty, joyous sound that echoed throughout the forlorn valley, the sudden expression of his lungs destroying his buoyancy, causing him to dip below the cold waters. He rose a moment later, coughing and laughing. His eyes were bleary from the silt of the pool and the salt of his own eyes, but Culp refused to blink, refused to take his eyes for one moment from his Captain.

In the mist, the shape of Sturmund lashed out, a series of thunderous blows that Culp heard even through the throbbing water at his ears.

Culp cried out to Sturmund, a shout of praise, a cheer, a farewell. Culp thought Sturmund had turned his head. He could imagine the eyes, proud and hard, looking down at his man from above, a look that said that Culp should steel himself, that the battle was never done.

And Sturmund struck again, the beast never giving any ground.

And the beast struck back, Sturmund never giving any ground.

Culp liked to think this, and as he cheered, he sank once below the water's surface and rose again no more.

OF STONE

The Keep had been built upon the highest mountain in the Northern range, a position chosen by the ancient builders for its strategic and symbolic value. At its back, desperate seas grappled with stony shores, a route impassible save for those already damned. At its fore, the vast expanse of kingdom stretched, friend and foe alike kept always in sight, always at arm's reach. At its heart, only hardness dwelt, for like its people, the core of the mountain offered nothing but stone. The grand cities of men and the wild lands of beast both groveled at the foot of a mountain, a monument, and a man.

∽

"I shall not forbid you." A dull band of gold rested upon a thinning mane; a heavy fur wrapped the broad shoulders and brushed the bare stone with each step. The lion spoke without once looking at the kneeling youth. Calm and steady came the voice, the true emotions buried as deep in lightless places as the hard rock on which his castle stood. "For I know you would defy, and I have no wish to kill you."

The blade that hung at the waist gleamed in the brilliant torchlight of the hall, the steel waking to the king's words. The monarch rested a hand against the itching hilt.

The supplicant did not stir at the challenge.

"This kingdom is your birthright," the monarch said, with the certainty of one unused to telling twice. "All the lands of north and south, from blackest sea to bluest ocean, every field and mountain between. Does it all mean so little to you?"

"It means everything to me, father." When the young man spoke, it was with an earnestness impossible to doubt. The sentiment, however, remained elusive. "That is why I can not rule."

Throughout the audience, the young man had not risen, his fair features buried against one knee. There he would remain until his lord wished otherwise. The king understood this, and his clever mind had considered leaving the boy there to grovel until the spirit faded and the will became more pliant. But a man knows his son, and though the knee might bend, the king recognized the heart never would.

So it was that with a long and searching look, the king who deferred to none, beseeched his child. "I never understand you, boy. Speak plainly to an old man, for my mind grows dull with the years. And get up off your knee."

"You are as sharp as your blade, father," the youth said, rising just as tall as his father, though scarcely half as wide. "It is your ears that refuse to hear."

"Then make them hear. Help them to understand." The king drew the boy to the fireside, where two chairs stood, one far more elaborate than the other, and father and son took their familiar places.

"This is no life for me, father. Where I am known by all and yet by none."

"Then go south, where they hardly know our names, let alone speak them."

"Perhaps I will, but it shall not be as prince, not as heir of anything except what I can earn with my hands and with my sword."

The father saw the strange passions gleam in the blue eyes, and at that moment knew he had lost his son. It would be some minutes more before his heart accepted such as well.

"Every lord, merchant, and peasant in the whole of this kingdom, in all the land that touches ocean wave, owes to you a debt of service, a bent knee, a bowed head. That is what you have earned, what our noble line has earned."

The young features hardened in distaste. "There is no honor in that, allegiance offered from fear or blind duty. It must be earned by deed, or it is valueless."

"And you think me so unworthy?" The fire beside them burned with less heat than did the boy's father at that moment. "That I have done so little to deserve this crown?"

"No, father," the boy said. "You simply do not understand, and I fear you never will."

"Then, go." The words came simply and softly, but their finality was undeniable.

"Father, I—" It would be the first time the boy would know true loss, true sacrifice. It would not be the last.

"I do not hate you, neither can I call you any son of mine. To deny your inheritance, to shirk the responsibility that countless of our line have nobly borne, to—" Here the king faltered, his passions slipping his stony grip. Finally, he said, "Your path strikes out along different roads, and its course cuts through my very heart. Go now, son. Live well, and never return."

They were the last words the boy would ever have of his father; and the last sight of the king, before the youth retired from the hall, was of an old man, sitting not upon his throne, but in the simple chair by the fire, where he remained, head in hands.

The king called for his steward and gave the bowing figure his instructions. The servant bowed once more at the door and disappeared, leaving the lion to his thoughts.

The hours passed as the king waited, and in that brooding silence it seemed to him, not for the first time, that it was not he who sat atop the heights of stone, but the mountain itself which weighed on his tired head. In the midst of such despondency, the doors opened and the steward reappeared. The man who followed with him brought comfort to the king's tired heart.

The years had not aged him; the king was not surprised to find it so. And when the man spoke, it was in the same beautiful tones that had warmed the hearts of so many women and softened the ire of even the most implacable foe.

"My king," the handsome man said, dropping gracefully to one knee, raven hair flowing off strong shoulders, his lithe body bending as humbly as if falling to prayer.

"Rise, old friend, and let me look upon a face familiar."

The figure rose at once, his soldier's armor shining brilliantly, the polished face mirroring all the golden splendor of the king's hall and still falling short of the brightness in the soldier's eyes.

The king took the soldier's face between hands still rough despite the years since they had last heaved the sword.

"Yes," the king said, his voice solemn as he appraised his visitor, "absolutely hideous."

The soldier stifled his laugh until leave were given, the creases of the eyes standing in stead of his lively voice.

The old lion roared then, a hearty laugh that set the guest to laughter as well. The king slapped his man on one arm and beckoned him join him at his table.

"A few good kisses of the sword would do well for your features," the king said, sitting his guest before himself. "You're much too pretty, Marney."

"If the blades could ever catch me," the soldier said, "I should welcome their rebuke."

"That day comes for us all, old friend," the king said, suddenly very grave. "I hope yours is a long way off yet."

The soldier nodded.

"I am pleased to find you here," the king continued, matters of business now at hand. "I had not thought to receive you so soon."

"It was strange chance, sire. These eleven years I have been in the South. Only my service papers have called me back, for I must reenlist in your majesty's forces before I may exercise your authority in the South."

"Then the gods favor us. What work was it has kept you so far from home all these years?" The king's cheek reddened at the subject, at his ignorance, and the soldier feigned not to notice.

"I have been stationed in the Lowlands, sire, driving out the bandits that plague the villages there. It is like cutting off demons' heads," the soldier said, warming easily to the topic, "from one springs many. We kill one bandit-king, and two more rise up in other towns. So we build outposts, train troops to man them. That is, when we can find enough—"

"This is not work befitting the hero of the Citadel." The king rose, his face flushed. "I owe you my life."

Marney fell from his chair and knelt at the foot of his lord. "My king, it is I who serve you. Your Majesty owes nothing to a humble soldier."

"Damn my shame," the king said. "That I have been too proud to honor you as you deserve. That every man and child in this kingdom does not know your name, let alone sing of it."

"You have honored me beyond measure, my lord, by allowing me to remain in your service after having disobeyed your orders."

"My orders." The king scoffed. "We should have no kingdom to call our own had my orders been obeyed, had not at least one soldier the guts and the balls to do what I ... what I should have done much sooner." Disgust and shame mingled in the old king's heart, and the resulting poison was anger; it sloshed inside his gut, and spilled from his mouth.

"And what does the hero of the Citadel earn from the hands of a thankful king?" The king raged, at Marney, at himself, at the halls and the mountain. "A pissing backwater and rodent-duty."

The anger flared, and the anger faded. The king dropped to his seat, defeated, his fires spent. The soldier remained at his feet.

"Please," the king said, urging his soldier to rise and retake his seat beside him, but the man held fast to his fealty.

"I defied your orders, your Majesty," Marney said, his

graceful tones now firm, forceful, building. "I scaled those battlements with spear gripped between my teeth, broke every damn bone in my hands getting up there where no one else could. I killed twenty, thirty men to get to that throne room—"

"—Marney." A warning; a plea.

"—and that's where I slew your brother."

The king's face trembled, the color paled, no words came. An awful silence filled the hall.

"What I did, sire, I did for my kingdom and my king. And what I did," the soldier said, "I will spend the rest of my life repenting over, for I wronged you, my king."

The king shook his head, reached out an unsteady hand, but did not quite let the fingers touch the man's head so that the hand hovered as if in benediction. "You made me worthy."

The terrible hush upon the hall softened, for grace had driven out the spectre of despair.

"Come to reenlist in the service of your king." The king spoke suddenly, and with none of the uncertainty of the moments before. "You have not signed your papers, then?"

"I have not, your Majesty."

"Then there is still time," the king said. "Still time for me to make right the wrong."

The king did not give his soldier the opportunity to protest, as his open mouth wished so clearly to do.

"Rise, sir knight. There is much I would ask of you." The king gripped his soldier by the arm and hoisted him up from his knee. He would look his man in the eye. "I have no right to ask it, but I shall all the same. Know that the choice shall remain yours."

"My king," Marney said, lowering his head in deference.

"You are not acquainted with my son."

We Burn Our Dead

"I have not had that honor."

"You would like him, I think," the king and father said. "He, too, is a defiant one."

Marney was relieved to find no resentment in the words, and the tired eyes of the old lion even carried something of a lightness in them as he spoke.

"He is leaving me."

The soldier said nothing, merely waited, as was correct, for a father speaks of his son in his own time, on his own terms.

"He wishes to walk the way of the warrior," the father continued. "To earn his life from nothing, to snatch each day from greedy Death. He does not know how hard the way will be." The king lowered his voice. "But you do."

"How may I serve?"

"Watch after my son, Marney. Watch him grow, as I can not. Guide his path, for I fear it heads to a precipice." There came a moment's pause, and the king's gaze clouded as he looked out on perhaps the years to come. "And I would not have him fall."

"If the boy is proud as you say, he will not suffer my company. Not if I am meant to temper the flame."

"Then you must find cause to make yourself known and welcome to him. Watch him from afar, learn his ways, for years if you must—but when the time is right, join yourself to his cause, cleave to him and never falter. Do this service for your king . . . and your friend."

The soldier bowed, deeply as though weighted with the honor, and made to take his leave.

"Only, Marney?" The soldier turned. "Never let him know it was I who sent you."

The soldier nodded, bowed once more. Then stopped, and hesitated.

"My king," Marney said, struggling with the awkwardness. "What is the boy's name? I have never heard it spoken in the South."

"With good reason, I expect." The king sighed.

"Sire?" The soldier struggled to recall.

"He had been named for his uncle."

When the fair-haired youth departed the castle walls for the last time, he did not look back. His black horse took him down the steep mountain pass at reckless pace to match the headstrong passion that drove it on.

Hours later, the gates opened once more, and the second rider departed. The man followed at some remove, his saddle laden with an uncommon number of supplies—texts and charts, tonics and spirits, coin and cutlass. He did not yet know what was to be required of him in his service; he knew only that the road ahead would be a long one, and as the miles lay unknown, one did well to be prepared.

45

There is a hillside by the sea not far from the site of a ruined village, the burnt timbers and gutted houses marking some forgotten battle. On that hill, overlooking the ocean, stands a mound of dirt atop which, over many long years, the grass has overcome and packed down. A man lies there who once walked the warrior's path, and who walks it still into eternity. His name is forgotten, his deeds along with it, but that is not important. There once lived men, brothers, strangers, who knew the man, fought with him and respected him.

That is all that matters.

In the woods nearby, deep in some overgrown copse where the forest holds dominion, are other graves. These patches of ground lie unmarked, memorialized by no one and nothing, but they exist despite this, and always shall.

WARRIOR'S PATH

"Seven came to the hill that day, killers and soldiers, mercenaries and cutthroats. The path they had followed stretched back many hard years, from points obscure, along varied and winding trails. Much was left unsaid; more left unfinished. But one thing remains certain: it ended at the hill, ended with the beast.

"Yet the ones who fell that day are not the ones who began their journey. Those that lie in the cold of that earth repose as warriors; who they were before, merely men. And that is where the story turns.

"Their path remains, and always shall. It is there, waiting: for those bold few with eyes that do not blink; hearts that do not quaver; feet that dare to tread; and minds that wish to know.

"The seven are dead, but their stories shall never lie quietly. One need only turn one's eyes to the past, and the sagas shall unfold."

Thus, the bard ended his tale, with an impressive sweep of his arm: raveling up the threads of story, calling back the listeners from their reverie, leaving only astonished silence in the wake of his practiced words.

A thoughtful, biding stillness lingered, wrapping the listeners in its thrall, as they considered something of their own lives and the decided absence of anything remotely heroic therein. As they dwelt with no small regret on the choices that had led them each to their mundane lots, the drinkers and diners, traveling merchants and brow-beaten husbands, clung fast and clumsily to the story's quickly fading warmth, blind men grasping water in their small fists. They thought wistfully of the tales that might be told of any of them, shamefully of the truths that certainly would be told of all of them; they considered the different paths they might have travelled to have raised them above their plodding desperation, and the decisions—more often the indecisions—that ensured they never would.

It was then that the storyteller, spying his moment with a practiced eye, chanced to clear his throat and nudge the cap he had laid by his travel-worn boots. Whether memories of long-forgotten childhood fancies or simple pity for a haggard old teller of tales informed the toss of copper, it was at this point the spare coins usually flowed—usually.

"Oh, come off it, old man," the drunkard said, breaking the spell and waking the last of the poor dreamers to the paltry light of each his own life. A fair bit younger in years than the rest of his fellow patrons, the rascal clearly had a mind to make up for his worldly inexperience with sheer volume. "You can't expect us to believe a one of those tired old tales. Why, this very evening, in a hundred inns across a hundred towns in this kingdom, some other bard is spinning yarns about other bleedin' heroes and other doofin' beasts."

The storyteller eyed the boy. He was not angry, nor

surprised; mere resignation colored the bard's features and his thoughts. So he would go hungry another night; it was no less than he deserved—not with the life he had led. Besides, he was not a one for heavy meals any more.

The bard's stomach churned painfully with a distant memory and an ever-present regret. He let the boy ramble on and readied himself once again for the road.

"Who among us," the rascal continued, appealing now to his companions, whose looks ranged from the bemused to the dangerously irritable, "has ever—and I mean even one fucking time—met anyone worthy of being called great, noble, or, hell, even half-way decent? Hmm? Speak up." At this, the youth cupped one ear to better hear his grumbling companions. "That's what I thought. All a bunch of pig's piss, and I don't mine telling you so. Life's shit and then you die. That's what I've learned in my seventeen years in this god-forsaken kingdom, and that's good enough for me. Now, wench! Bring me another ale."

And with this, the boy sat, his peroration drawing as many jeers as half-hearted applause. Beer once more began to flow, and the bard was all but forgotten as he packed his bindle. Not in long minutes had a man among them cast a glance over to the open door, outside of which the ruddy afternoon had long since slipped to balmy evening, the slow breeze that drifted in a welcome relief after so hot a day.

Not a man among them, then, had seen the arrival of the stranger, appearing so suddenly and silently from the blackness outside that a drunker mind might have called it magic. But it was not magic, of course; it was skill.

The stranger stood in the doorway and waited; for what, was not immediately apparent.

When, at length, one of the patrons happened to glance up from his cups and see the stranger, he did not call out, as was the custom in their parts, to invite a weary traveler in from the road. He only stared at the figure in the doorway, saying not one word to him, and when his unblinking eyes might perhaps threaten impertinence to the stranger, merely shifted his gaze to the door frame, or to the spot of ceiling above the stranger's head, or to the floor beneath his feet. What he did not do, this mute drinker, was dare to turn his back on such a figure as had walked into his life.

A moment later another eye from the crowded barroom chanced to fall upon the figure in the doorway, and another voice fell silent. Soon another, and another still, until eventually every single man among them had raised his eyes or shifted in his seat, his arm thrown round his chair back, his leg swung over his stool or bench, to turn and behold the presence that loomed so impossibly large, for there was something in the stranger's eye that stifled the voice, an absolute hardness against which idle glances struck and fell away from bashfully.

It was then that the bard turned.

"Sinner."

The bard did not seem much surprised to see his erstwhile brother. The name came wearily from his lips, as though he already felt the burden that had not yet been given voice, but did not lack for weight.

"The witch," Sinner said, wild eyes burning.

At the word, Strange Bob, for so the bard could only be, grabbed his withered gut, terrible memories of the poison and the curse they had suffered so many moons ago returning like the pox—dormant, but never forgotten.

"It is as she said," the long-absent brother continued, "on her dying breath—she has returned."

The onlookers were seized by confusion and doubt at the scene, unsure of their footing, wary of a grift, but with mouths wise enough to stay shut. Caution possessed a lesser hold on the rascal, however, whose inexperience gleamed like honey to the stinging bees. The youth stared between the two old men, until finally, shit met grin, and tongue found voice. "Oh, give me a fucking brea—"

Lightening flared outside the inn, breaking from utter stillness and setting the world aglow in uncanny fire. In the distance, a woman wailed, baleful and malicious, a cry that gripped the heart and wrung from it every drop of hope, every forgotten word of prayer.

The last thing the young rascal saw before passing out—and the first thing he recalled upon waking to piss-damp trousers—was this: an aged bard drawing a cruel blade from out his robe faster and with more skill than any soldier half his age had any right; an old storyteller with eyes of fire and a heart of stone, flying from the inn, fearsome companion at his side; two brothers setting off into the yawning night and all its terrors, the world of mere men left far behind them, a warrior's path stretching far ahead.

If a man can breathe...

Made in United States
Orlando, FL
28 June 2025